AB

Barbara Cartland, th
who is also an histor
and television person
sold over 600 million

She has also had
written four autobiographies as well as the ~~biog~~
mother and that of her brother, Ronald Cartland, who was the
first Member of Parliament to be killed in the last war. This book
has a preface by Sir Winston Churchill and has just been
published with an introduction by the late Sir Arthur Bryant.

"Love at the Helm" a novel written with the help and
inspiration of the late Earl Mountbatten of Burma, Great Uncle
of His Royal Highness The Prince of Wales, is being sold for the
Mountbatten Memorial Trust.

She has broken the world record for the last nineteen years by
writing an average of twenty-three books a year. In the Guinness
Book of Records she is listed as the world's top-selling author.

In 1978 she sang an Album of Love Songs with the Royal
Philharmonic Orchestra.

In private life Barbara Cartland, who is a Dame of Grace of
the Order of St John of Jerusalem, Chairman of the St John
Council in Hertfordshire and Deputy President of the St John
Ambulance Brigade, has fought for better conditions and salaries
for Midwives and Nurses.

She championed the cause for the Elderly in 1956 invoking a
Government Enquiry into the "Housing Conditions of Old
People".

In 1962 she had the Law of England changed so that Local
Authorities had to provide camps for their own Gypsies. This
has meant that since then thousands and thousands of Gypsy
children have been able to go to School which they had never
been able to do in the past, as their caravans were moved every
twenty-four hours by the Police.

There are now fourteen camps in Hertfordshire and Barbara
Cartland has her own Romany Gypsy Camp called Barbaraville
by the Gypsies.

Her designs "Decorating with Love" are being sold all over the USA and the National Home Fashions League made her in 1981 "Woman of Achievement".

Barbara Cartland's book "Getting Older, Growing Younger" has been published in Great Britain and the USA and her fifth Cookery Book, "The Romance of Food" is now being used by the House of Commons.

In 1984 she received at Kennedy Airport, America's Bishop Wright Air Industry Award for her contribution to the development of aviation. In 1931 she and two RAF Officers thought of, and carried, the first aeroplane-towed glider air-mail.

During the War she was Chief Lady Welfare Officer in Bedfordshire looking after 20,000 Service men and women. She thought of having a pool of Wedding Dresses at the War Office so a Service Bride could hire a gown for the day.

She bought 1,000 secondhand gowns without coupons for the ATS, the WAAFS and the WRENS. In 1945 Barbara Cartland received the Certificate of Merit from Eastern Command.

In 1964 Barbara Cartland founded the National Association for Health of which she is the President, as a front for all the Health Stores and for any product made as alternative medicine.

This has now a £600,000,000 turnover a year, with one third going in export.

In January 1988 she received "La Medaille de Vermeil de la Ville de Paris", (The Gold Medal of Paris). This is the highest award to be given by the City of Paris for ACHIEVEMENT – 25 million books sold in France.

In March 1988 Barbara Cartland was asked by the Indian Government to open their Health Resort outside Delhi. This is almost the largest Health Resort in the world.

Barbara Cartland was received with great enthusiasm by her fans, who also fêted her at a Reception in the City and she received the gift of an embossed plate from the Government.

Barbara Cartland was made a Dame of the Order of the British Empire in the 1991 New Year's Honours List, by Her Majesty The Queen, for her contribution to literature and for her work for the Community.

Dame Barbara has now written the greatest number of books by a British author, passing the 564 books written by John Creasey.

AWARDS

1945   Received Certificate of Merit, Eastern Command.

1953   Made a Commander of the Order of St John of Jerusalem. Invested by H.R.H. The Duke of Gloucester at Buckingham Palace.

1972   Invested as Dame of Grace of the Order of St John in London by The Lord Prior, Lord Cacia.

1981   Receives "Achiever of the Year" from the National Home Furnishing Association in Colorado Springs, U.S.A.

1984   Receives Bishop Wright Air Industry Award at Kennedy Airport, for inventing the aeroplane-towed Glider.

1988   Receives from Monsieur Chirac, The Prime Minister, the Gold Medal of the City of Paris, at the Hôtel de la Ville, Paris, for selling 25 million books and giving a lot of employment.

1991   Invested as Dame of the Order of The British Empire, by H.M. The Queen at Buckingham Palace, for her contribution to literature.

A Dog, a Horse and a Heart

When Manella's Uncle, the Earl of Avondale tells her that he is selling her beloved horse *Heron*, and her dog *Flash*, she is heartbroken.

Then when he says she is to marry an elderly Peer, the Duke of Dunster she is horrified.

At daybreak she rides away on *Heron* with *Flash* at her heels, not knowing where to go.

Arriving at a little village she stops for some food and learns that the Marquis of Buckingdon is coming home with a party of friends and the Cook has had a stroke.

Because her Grandmother, who was French, taught her how to make French dishes, and she knows she is a good cook, Manella offers to take her place until she is better.

How Manella is bribed to help a Frenchman play a joke on the Marquis.

How she 'turns the tables' on his friends and cooks him a special 'Hero's Speciality'.

How once again she saves the Marquis when *Flash* warns her of danger is all told in this fascinating story, the 499th by Barbara Cartland.

BARBARA CARTLAND

A Dog, a Horse and a Heart

Mandarin

A Mandarin Paperback

A DOG, A HORSE AND A HEART

First published in Great Britain 1994
by Mandarin Paperbacks
an imprint of Reed Consumer Books Ltd
Michelin House, 81 Fulham Road, London SW3 6RB
and Auckland, Melbourne, Singapore and Toronto

Copyright © Cartland Promotions 1994
The author has asserted her moral rights

A CIP catalogue record for this title
is available from the British Library

ISBN 0 7493 1280 7

Printed and bound in Great Britain
by Cox & Wyman Ltd, Reading, Berks

AUTHOR'S NOTE

The Setter Hunting Dog has been known and used in England for at least four hundred years.

The name 'Setter' is derived from the verb 'to set' which means to stiffen, position and point.

The name is therefore indicative of the role of the Setter as a pointing dog, although it adopts a different posture from the Pointer.

The Setter hunts with its head held high in order not to miss the faintest scent of bird game.

The most ancient Setter breed is the English Setter, evolved from crosses between the Spanish Pointer and Springer Spaniel.

It was first bred by Sir Edward Laverack in the early nineteenth century.

The English Setter is an excellent hunting dog, good on any ground, whether it be flat land or marsh, woods or bush.

In appearance, it is extremely attractive, elegant, well balanced and powerful without being heavy.

Its coat is long, silky fine and slightly wavy, short on the head with abundant feathering at the legs.

The name 'Marquess' or 'Marquis', has the same meaning as Margrave, but this original significance has long been lost.

It was in 1385 that Robert de Vere, 9th Earl of Oxford, was created Marquess of Dublin with precedence between Dukes and Earls.

This was resented by other Earls and the patent of the Marquessate was revoked on October 13th, 1386, after its holder had been created Duke of Ireland.

John Beaufort, Earl of Somerset objected to being created a Marquess in 1402 because of the strangeness of the term in England.

On June 24th, 1443, however, his son Edmund Beaufort was raised to be Marquess of Dorset, after which the title retained its place in the Peerage.

CHAPTER ONE
1819

"I have sold that dog," the Earl said.

For a moment Manella looked at him in astonishment.

Then she asked:

"What do you mean, Uncle Herbert? You cannot have sold *Flash*? It could not be true!"

"Your Father took him shooting with Lord Lambourne last year, I am told, and Lambourne was extremely impressed that he was so fast and obedient."

"My Father was very fond of *Flash*," Manella replied, "but he is my dog. He belongs to me."

Her Uncle gave her a searching look before he asked:

"You have that in writing?"

"No, of course not," Manella answered. "Is it likely that Papa would write down what he had given me? But *Flash* has always been mine."

"You will not want him with you in London," the Earl said. "So Lambourne is coming to fetch him tomorrow afternoon."

Manella gave a cry.

"You cannot . . you cannot do this to me, Uncle Herbert! I refuse to allow it and I will . . not lose *Flash*!"

The Earl of Avondale walked across the room to stand in front of the fireplace.

"Now, let us get this clear, Manella," he said. "Your Father left very little money and you are now my responsibility. You will appreciate that therefore I am doing what is best for you."

Manella did not reply and her Uncle went on:

"I have gone to a great deal of trouble already to arrange that you shall have a Season in London, and the Duchess of Westmoore will chaperon you."

Vaguely, at the back of her mind, Manella remembered that the Duchess of Westmoore was very beautiful.

She had heard her Father remark that his brother Herbert was 'making a fool of himself over her'.

She did not say anything aloud, and the Earl went on:

"Most girls would be jumping for joy at the idea of being chaperoned by a Duchesss. And I have also, I think, found you a husband."

Manella drew in a deep breath.

"I do not mean to be rude, Uncle Herbert," she said, "but I do not want my husband, when I have one, found for me. I wish to marry someone I love."

The Earl laughed and it was not a very humorous sound.

"'Beggars cannot be choosers', my dear niece," he replied. "I happened to be in White's Club last week when the Duke of Dunster came in."

"The Duke of Dunster was a friend of Papa's," Manella interposed.

"I know that," the Earl replied, "and I also know that he would give anything in the world to have a son to succeed him."

"I can hardly . . believe you are . . considering the . . Duke as my . . husband," Manella said hesitatingly. "He is old . . very old."

"What has that got to do with it?" the Earl enquired. "He is a Duke, he is rich and, if you are lucky enough to marry him, your whole future is made for you."

"I think you must be mad," Manella retorted, "if you think I would consider . . marrying a man who is . . old enough to be my . . Grandfather."

"I know the Duke has admitted that he can no longer shoot. But his son can do that, when he has one," the Earl replied. "Before you give me any more of your cheek, let me point out, Manella, that as I am your Guardian, you have to obey me, and if I tell you that you are to marry the Duke, you will marry him!"

"In which case you will have to drag me to the altar, and I assure you that once I am there I will refuse to take part in the Marriage Service!" Manella said furiously.

There was an ominous look in her Uncle's eyes as he said:

"The trouble with you, Manella, is that you have been spoilt. You are a pretty girl, I will not argue about that. But unless you want to starve and be left without a penny to your name, you will do exactly what I tell you to do, and immediately!"

He walked across the room to the door.

"I am going now to inform Glover that Lord Lambourne will be here tomorrow afternoon. He will collect *Flash*, and I hope I will be able to sell him at least two horses. The rest are only fit for the Butcher's."

He went out of the room as he finished speaking, shutting the door noisily behind him.

For a moment Manella could only stare after him.

She could not believe what she had heard, could not credit that it was the truth and she was not dreaming.

How was it possible that her father's brother could behave in such a heartless and cruel way?

How could he take away *Flash*, whom she loved and who had been with her ever since he was a puppy?

He had grown into a very fine Setter. He was powerful but elegant. His white coat flecked with black was fine and silky and slightly wavy and he was admired by everyone who saw him.

He followed her about the house, slept in her bedroom, and in fact went everywhere that she went.

It had never occurred to her when her Uncle had said they were going to London that she would not be able to take *Flash* with her.

Now she was not only to lose the house where she had been born and where she had lived ever since.

She was also to lose *Flash* and *Heron*, the horse that she had always ridden and had believed was also hers.

She knew only too well there were only two horses in the stables in which Lord Lambourne was likely to be interested.

One of them was *Heron*.

On top of all this, her Uncle was talking about her being married, but not to a man whom she might love.

He wanted her to marry a decrepit old man who wanted a wife only in order to have a son.

The horror of it swept over her like a tidal wave and she wanted to scream and go on screaming.

Then she told herself that she must keep her self-control.

She must try to find some escape from the horrible, ghastly mist in which she felt she was being suffocated.

She looked up at the portrait over the mantelpiece which was of her Father.

It had been painted when he was a young man by one of the great Artists who had painted the Prince of Wales before he became the Prince Regent.

The 6th Earl of Avondale, her Father looked extremely distinguished and, as she told herself, very much a Gentleman.

That was something her Uncle certainly was not, and never had been.

It had often struck her in the past what an extraordinary difference there was between her Father and his younger brother, her Uncle.

She remembered once, when a large bill was sent to him because his brother had failed to settle it, her Father saying:

"I suppose there is a 'Black Sheep' in every family, but Herbert is certainly proving himself blacker than most!"

Somehow the Earl had managed to pay his brother's debts, and it was not for the first, or the last time.

It was in fact largely due to Herbert's extravagance that they were so hard up.

The war had certainly made things very difficult.

A number of those who had rented houses had left them because they were too large.

Or else they could not pay even the reasonable rent the Earl asked.

At the same time, the farms did well because there were no foreign imports coming onto the market.

England therefore had to be self-supporting.

But as soon as the war was over, the Farmers 'felt the pinch'.

A number of County Banks had even closed their doors.

'If only Papa had not died just at this moment,' Manella thought despairingly.

He had suffered an unexpected heart-attack early last Autumn.

Herbert, the 'Black Sheep', the ne'er-do-well, had come into the title.

Because he had expected to have to wait many years before this happened, he had great difficulty in looking solemn and sad at the Funeral.

There had always been the possibility too that his brother might marry again and produce an heir.

But he was now the Earl!

As soon as the Funeral was over, Herbert had started looking around the house for something to sell.

But most of the pictures and the furniture were entailed onto each succeeding Earl, whoever he might be.

Herbert had said to Manella without the slightest hint of embarrassment:

"I now have the opportunity of finding myself a rich bride."

Manella said nothing and he looked at her with a sneer on his lips and he added:

"You need not be so hoity-toity! You know as well as I do that your Father was 'down to bed-rock', which is something I have been for years and years!"

He was silent for a moment before he went on:

"But an Earl, poor or not, is a very different story from a younger son with no prospects!"

"Then I hope, Uncle Herbert," Manella said stiffly, "that you will find someone with whom you can be happy."

"I will be happy with anyone, providing she is rich enough!" her Uncle replied.

He had gone back to London, taking with him a number of items he intended to sell.

There was some Sèvres china of which her Mother had always been very fond.

Manella tried to prevent him from removing it from the house.

"Now do not be stupid," her Uncle objected. "You know I need money, and it is for your benefit rather than mine that I intend to open Avondale House in Berkeley Square."

Manella looked at him in astonishment.

"How can you afford to do that?" she asked. "Papa always said it was terribly expensive to keep up and needed a great number of servants."

"I am well aware of that," her Uncle admitted, "but I shall be closing this house, leaving only a skeleton staff, just in case I wish to give a party here."

He saw the consternation in Manella's face and added:

"Of course I will have to impress my rich bride with the ancestral home of the Earls of Avondale."

He had stayed in London for so long that Manella began to hope that what he had been saying was a lot of nonsense.

Alternatively, perhaps he was finding that it was not as easy to capture a rich bride as he had expected it to be.

Then yesterday he had returned unexpectedly.

Manella felt herself shrink from him the moment he walked into the house.

He did not look in the least like her Father.

She had always thought there was something insignificant as well as unpleasant about her Uncle.

The moment he appeared, she was aware that he was extremely smartly dressed.

He had arrived in a Phaeton that looked new and expensive and the horses pulling it were well bred.

She hoped, as he stepped in through the front door, that he had found his rich bride-to-be.

Once that happened, she thought she would see as little of him as possible.

Now he had dropped a bomb-shell.

She found it difficult to think clearly after the shock of what he had just said.

Flash was lying on the hearthrug and she dropped down on her knees and put her arms round him.

"I cannot lose you . ., I cannot!" she said in a broken voice. "And I have always heard that Lord Lambourne is hard on his horses and his dogs. Oh, *Flash*, *Flash*, how could I . . sleep at night if I thought you were in some . . cold kennel and could not . . understand why I was . . not with . . you?'

It was then the tears rolled down her cheeks and she brushed them away impatiently.

"I have to think what we can do. Oh, *Flash*, tell me what we can do."

Because the dog understood that she was distressed, he licked her face.

Then he nuzzled her arm so that she put it round him.

She held him close and said through her tears:

"I cannot lose you . . I cannot! If I have to . . go to London and . . marry some horrible old man . . I will die!"

She thought even to herself it sounded too melodramatic, and yet she knew it was the truth.

How could she live knowing that *Flash* and *Heron* no longer belonged to her?

It was bad enough losing first her Mother and then her Father whom she had loved.

She had thought when he died that life stood still.

The future was dark.

But even in her worst fears of what her Uncle Herbert might do, it had never struck her for a moment she would be separated from the two animals she loved more than anything else in the world.

Or that she would be taken to London, to be disposed of to a husband he chose!

She was not even to be consulted.

"I will . . not do it . . I will not!" she declared.

She sat back on her heels and looked up at her Father's portrait.

Because of the way she had spoken and because she had released him, *Flash* thought it meant they were going for a walk.

Jumping up, he ran towards the door.

As he did so, Manella said:

"You are telling me what to do! Oh, *Flash*, how clever of you! Why did I not think of that myself?"

She jumped to her feet and opened the door of the Study.

Flash went out first, running ahead.

It was then Manella began to plan her escape.

She was trying to keep calm and not be so apprehensive that she could not think clearly.

She realised it would be a problem to earn enough money to live on her own.

She would also have to hide so cleverly that her Uncle would never find her.

Manella went to her bed-room.

Sitting down at the dressing-table, she looked at herself in the mirror.

It was almost as if she was asking her reflection to guide her.

Manella had lived in the country all her life.

During the war they had few neighbours and practically no parties.

She was therefore quite unaware of how outstandingly pretty, in fact lovely, she was.

She was completely unselfconscious about herself.

Soon after her Father's death she had seen her Uncle looking at her critically.

"You are making me feel uncomfortable, Uncle Herbert!" she said. "Have I a smut on the end of my nose?"

"I was just thinking," the new 7th Earl of Avondale had replied slowly, "that you are a pretty young woman. In fact you compare very favourably with the portraits of the Countesses of Avondale who were always considered Beauties in whatever period they lived."

Manella had been surprised, but she had said a little shyly:

"Thank you, Uncle Herbert. I think that is the first compliment you have ever paid me."

He did not answer.

There was a look in his eyes which somehow made her feel apprehensive.

She had the strange feeling that he was thinking her looks were an asset in some way she could not understand.

Now she realised that if she had a rich and important husband, it would be an asset to him.

An asset which was obviously of importance in Society, besides of course, money.

How often, Manella remembered, had her Father said:

"Why my brother wants to live in London I cannot imagine! But he has always been the same. Never cared for the country, never had any country interests, and was always a bad shot."

That, Manella knew, condemned him in her Father's eyes.

He expected every English Gentleman to enjoy the country and country sports.

He should want to ride the best horses and shoot the highest birds.

Sometimes, when some of their relations came to stay, Manella would hear them talking to her Father about his brother in low voices.

She had not been particularly interested.

But as they sat in one of the smaller rooms, if there was not a big party, she could not help overhearing their comments about Herbert's extravagance.

They also had a great deal to say about his many love-affairs.

What concerned her Father more than anything else was his brother's debts.

The debts that were always brought to him for settlement when it was impossible for Herbert to pay what he owed.

It was a question for the Earl of either finding the money or letting Herbert rot in a Debtors' Prison.

Manella was well aware of how much her Father had suffered from this continual drain on the comparatively small amount of money he possessed.

It meant that he could not have the horses he wanted, or that another game-keeper had to be dismissed.

Or that urgent repairs to the house could not be undertaken, even though the rain came through the roof.

"Why do you keep doing this for Uncle Herbert?" Manella had asked her Father once.

He had smiled somewhat drily as he replied:

"'Blood is thicker than water', my dear, and however tiresome Herbert may be, he is my brother, and I have a deep regard for the family name."

This meant that he could not allow Herbert to go to prison.

Manella knew that this was what her Uncle Herbert had always counted on.

'I hate him! I hate him!' she thought as she looked at her reflection in the mirror.

She was thinking that she had somehow to earn enough money to live, and wondered what she could do.

Her hair was the pale gold of the sun in the early morning.

Her eyes, instead of being blue as might have been expected because she was English, were the green of a woodland stream.

There was just a touch of gold in them which looked like the sun reflected on the water.

One of the maids had once told her that she had a heart-shaped face.

When she looked at it she knew it was the truth.

Her eyes were very large and, strangely enough, her eye-lashes were dark.

This was due, her Father had always said, to a Spanish ancestress who had married one of the first Earls of Avondale.

Unfortunately there was no portrait of this particular Countess, and Manella often thought it was sad that she had been omitted.

She thought perhaps it was because the family had not liked her.

There was another foreigner who had more recently graced the Family Tree, and that was Manella's Grandmother, who had been French.

Manella had thought how much it must have hurt her to know that her country was at war with her country of adoption.

However according to her Diary, she had been extremely happy.

She was not dark, as might have been expected, of a Frenchwoman but, having come from Normandy, she was fair.

Only her eyes showed that she was definitely not English.

It was her Grandmother who had taught Manella to speak French when she was small.

Because of this she found it as easy to read a book in French as one in English.

"I am sure, Grandmama," she had said when Napoleon was raging about the Continent, and threatening to invade England, "that I should not speak the language of our enemy."

"You never know when it might come in useful," her Grandmother had argued. "It is my opinion that the English make a great mistake in thinking they should not speak any language but their own. Whether they like it or not, they have to associate with other countries in Europe."

Manella had to admit that this was true.

She therefore continued to speak French with her Grandmother and to read the books written in French that she lent her.

Her Grandmother had gone out of her way to be kind to the French *émigrés* who had come to England.

Most of them had not returned to France during the Armistice despite the fact that Napoleon had said he would welcome them.

When war had broken out again in 1804 they had been thankful that they had not taken advantage of his invitation.

"The man is an upstart – a discredit to his race!" Manella's Grandmother had said scornfully.

She had been very outspoken and in many ways had a positive personality that was unusual.

Manella sat wondering how her Grandmother would act in her present circumstances.

She was quite certain she would not let herself be bullied into marrying anyone she did not wish to marry.

She would certainly not agree to *Flash* being sold.

"But what can I do? How can I prevent it?" Manella asked her reflection despairingly.

"*Flash* is right," she told herself finally. "I shall have to run away."

She spent the rest of the day trying to decide what she should take with her.

What was more important was how she could get enough money to save herself from starvation.

At least until she could find employment of some sort.

It was not going to be easy if she was to take *Heron* with her as well as her dog.

She could imagine what the housemaids at Avondale Hall would say if a servant arrived there with a well-bred horse and an outstanding Setter.

"I am sure something will turn up," Manella told herself consolingly.

At the same time she was frightened.

There would be a tremendous fuss when she ran away.

Then if she was caught and returned home ignominiously, she knew how her Uncle would jeer at her.

He would keep her, having failed to become independent, triumphantly 'under his thumb'.

She would have to do everything he told her to do.

Once again she thought of the Duke of Dunster and shivered.

She remembered her Father saying that he was now too old to take part in the shoots, and that old men could often be a danger to others.

If the Duke had been too old then, he was even older now.

How could she bear to be kissed, or even touched by an old man with white hair?

Since her Mother's death she had lived alone with her Father. So Manella was very innocent.

She had no idea what being married actually entailed.

She was of course aware that it was something intimate, and that married people shared a bed.

Her Mother had been deeply in love with her Father, and he with her.

Whenever he had been away from home for a day and came back, her Mother would run into the hall to greet him.

Regardless of the servants, who were in fact elderly and had been with them a long time, they would kiss each other lovingly.

Manella had been brought up in an atmosphere of love.

When she thought about marriage, which was not often, she imagined that the man she married would be tall and handsome like her Father.

She would look at him and her face would glow, as her Mother's did, so that she looked even more beautiful than usual.

"I have missed you," she had heard her Father say once. "A day without you, my Darling, is a very long day."

"And I have been counting the hours until your return," her Mother had replied.

As they looked at each other, Manella had been aware of the vibrations passing between them because they were so happy.

'That is how I want to feel,' she thought, 'and . . I will never, never marry anyone unless I feel like that!'

It was a vow she made to herself.

Then she started packing.

She knew that everything she carried had to be strapped to the back of *Heron*'s saddle.

There was room for slippers, if they were soft, in the pockets under the saddle.

She had to make the most of what little space there was.

As she thought it over, she decided she would not wear a habit.

She wanted clothes in which she could work without feeling uncomfortable or restricted.

She still could not think what employment she could find.

Yet when she went down to dinner with her Uncle, she knew that, if she had to scrub floors and sleep in an attic, it would be better than living with him or with a husband she did not love.

He had brought with him from London a certain amount of wine.

He had found when his brother died that the cellars were almost empty.

He had also ordered the servants to buy him something decent to eat for dinner, as Manella heard in surprise.

He had actually given them the money with which to buy it.

They had been scraping along since he had gone to London on rabbits which they caught in the woods.

There had been a duck or two which were to be found on the streams, and the eggs the chickens laid.

They roamed about in what had been known as the 'Kitchen Garden'.

They apparently found enough to eat there, for it was very seldom Manella could afford to buy any corn for them.

Somehow they had managed, although Manella was aware that she had lost a number of inches from her waist.

Emily, the housemaid, who was getting very old, had difficulty in sewing, and grumbled when she had to take her gowns in.

Her Uncle had also brought a pâté, and she felt he was watching her carefully to see how much she took.

She therefore restricted herself to just a very small piece of it.

"I knew I would get little or nothing to eat here!" the Earl said scornfully. "But I have engaged an excellent Cook for my house in Berkeley Square."

Manella noticed the word 'my'.

She knew how much her Father would despise his brother for closing their home in the country where the Earls of Avondale had lived for three hundred years.

Instead he was opening a house in London which was comparatively new, having been bought by his grandfather.

Her Uncle, following his own thoughts, was boasting:

"I intend to give some very smart parties," he was saying, "and of course, until you are married, you will help me to entertain."

He looked her up and down before he said:

"I suppose I shall have to find money for you to buy some decent clothes. You certainly cannot appear as you are now."

Manella raised her chin.

"Papa liked me in simple dresses," she said, "and although this one was made by the village seamstress, it is from a design which appeared in the *Ladies Journal*."

Her Uncle gave a rude laugh.

"If you think that would 'pass muster' in the *Beau Ton*," he said, "you are very much mistaken. In fact, if you want the truth, my dear niece, you look a mess! Your hair is not arranged in a fashionable manner, and your gown, if you appeared in it, would be laughed at from one end of Mayfair to the other!"

"I have no doubt you are right, Uncle Herbert," Manella said, "but Papa thought it wrong to buy anything, unless we could pay for it."

She hoped she would make him feel uncomfortable, but instead he only laughed.

"Your Father may have been content to let you rot here amongst the turnips," he said. "But I am taking you into the real world, the world of important people who will be of use to us both."

Manella knew he was speaking once again of the Duke, and she felt herself stiffen.

Then her Uncle said, looking at her in an appraising manner:

"Perhaps, after all, he will find it rather amusing to discover for himself that you are a 'Beauty'! At the same time, we cannot take the risk."

He paused before he said again:

"No, it would be too great a risk. I must have you properly dressed, your hair arranged, and perhaps a touch of salve on your lips to make them more inviting."

The way he spoke made Manella feel as if she was listening to the hiss of a serpent.

She wanted to rage at him that nothing would

make her try to attract the Duke or any man who did not love her for herself.

Then she knew it would be quite pointless to say anything like that to a man who was completely insensitive.

He looked at life merely as a means of benefiting him materially.

Manella put down the cup of coffee with which they had finished their dinner.

"I think, Uncle Herbert," she said, "if you will excuse me, it would be correct to leave you to your Port, if you have any."

"I am glad you have been taught some of the conventions," the Earl replied. "However, I am quite certain there are a great number you do not know."

Manella rose to her feet.

"I hope you will forgive me, Uncle Herbert," she said, "if I now go to bed. I shall have a great deal to do, if you are thinking of leaving for London the day after tomorrow."

"I suppose you will have to take some of those old rags you are wearing with you!" her Uncle replied. "As soon as the Duchess has found you some decent clothes, we can burn the lot – and a good thing too, if you ask me!"

How dare he be so scathing Manella thought.

It was almost entirely due to him that she had been unable to afford any new gowns for a long time!

How dare he criticise her for being a 'country

bumpkin' and unlike the women with whom he amused himself in London.

Women with whom he had caused, if she was not mistaken, scandal after scandal!

Pressing her lips together so as not to reply, Manella curtsied politely and turned towards the door.

"Do not forget that Lambourne is coming tomorrow," her Uncle said as she went out, "and you can give that dog a brushing. He looks as if he has just come out of the dustbin!"

Manella knew he was deliberately trying to provoke her.

Only as she ran up the stairs with *Flash* at her heels did she say over and over again beneath her breath:

"I hate . . him! I hate . . him! I hate . . him!"

CHAPTER TWO

The sun was just beginning to peep over the horizon when Manella got out of bed.

She had only slept for a short while, finding herself going over and over again in her mind what she had to do.

She dressed quickly, having the night before laid out the clothes she intended to put on.

She had wrapped those she was taking with her in a light shawl.

She had intended to take three of her simplest muslin gowns which she hoped would not get too creased and would last her through the Summer.

For the time being, she gave no thought to what would happen in the Winter.

Her riding-habit was warm and would be all she wanted if it rained.

She had two pairs of shoes that fitted into the saddle-pockets, and a few other small articles she knew she would need.

34

She had also late last night, when she thought her Uncle would be asleep, gone down to the Armoury to get one of her Father's duelling pistols.

She was not so foolish as not to realise that she might be waylaid by Highwaymen.

She would be carrying very little of value on her, but she was riding *Heron*.

She had heard that Highwaymen often took the best horses of anyone they held up.

Lastly, and it had taken her a long time to work it out, she had to have some ready money.

There was her Mother's jewellery, which was not very valuable.

It was what her Father had given her as presents, and it always upset him that he could not afford more expensive pieces.

Her Mother's engagement-ring was of diamonds, and there was also a diamond necklace that she had worn on special occasions.

The stones were not very large or fine.

But if she was desperate, Manella thought, it would fetch enough money to last her for a month or so.

What she lacked was cash.

She had only a few coins left from what she had been using as housekeeping money.

She had lain awake thinking what she could do.

Then she remembered that yesterday her Uncle had given Mrs. Bell the Cook several guineas.

This was not her wages, which were overdue, but

money to buy what he had called a 'proper meal' for Lord Lambourne.

"I have sent a groom to ask His Lordship to come to luncheon," he said. "I intend to give him a bottle of my best wine, and I want you to serve a proper meal and not the rubbish you gave me last night and this morning, which is only fit for the pigs!"

Manella thought it was a very unkind and unfair thing to say to Mrs. Bell.

She had done her best to provide them with food without spending a penny more than was absolutely necessary.

She saw the elderly woman flush, but she did not speak and her Uncle said aggressively:

"Buy a leg of young lamb, and some cheese that does not look as if it is only fit for the rats!"

He paused before he added:

"I suppose we had better have some fruit. Strawberries or raspberries will do, and I expect you will have to buy those too."

He walked out of the Kitchen as he finished speaking.

Manella realised that Mrs. Bell was muttering beneath her breath.

"I am sorry, Mrs. Bell," she said softly. "Uncle Herbert had no right to speak to you like that!"

"I've done me best, M'Lady, as you well knows," Mrs. Bell said, "but I can't make bricks wi'out straw, an' that's the truth!"

"Of course it is," Manella said consolingly, "but we all know what Uncle Herbert is like."

She sighed before she went on:

"I suppose now that he has become an Earl he is able to borrow money which he has not been able to do before."

She was speaking more to herself than to Mrs. Bell, but the elderly woman said:

"I 'ears from the groom that's with 'is Lordship that 'e's got debts a mile long! But 'e's promised them as is asking for settlement that they'll all be met in under a month."

Manella stared at Mrs. Bell in astonishment.

"How is that possible?" she asked.

"The groom didn't know that. But 'e says 'e thought it were somethin' to do wi' a weddin'."

Manella started.

She knew only too well whose wedding that would be.

As she had guessed, her Uncle intended to put pressure on the Duke, once he was her husband.

He would behave in exactly the same way as he had to her Father.

He used to point out the danger of a scandal which would affect the whole family.

He had been quite confident in his crafty, cunning mind that his brother would pay up.

Now, Manella thought, he intended to transfer these methods to the Duke.

He of course would not want a scandal that would involve his wife.

She went into the Kitchen knowing where Mrs. Bell always kept the housekeeping money.

It was in a tin that stood on the dresser.

When she pulled off the lid she found, as she expected, that there were two golden guineas untouched.

There was also quite a lot of small change.

She took it all, then put a note which she had already written to her Uncle propped up on the dresser.

She wanted Mrs. Bell to find it there before she discovered that the money was missing.

The note was short, and she thought that for the moment it would prevent her Uncle from realising she had run away.

She wrote:

"Dear Uncle Herbert,

After you had gone to bed last night, I received a message from one of my friends inviting me to go and stay with her for a party they are giving tomorrow-night.

As I am very anxious to be present, I am riding over there on Heron. I am also taking Flash with me.

Lord Lambourne may be disappointed, but I expect you will be able to console him, and he can always call another day.

As I needed some money to take with me, I have taken what you gave Mrs. Bell for the food, so you must not blame her if you have to give her more for anything you require.

I shall be returning soon, but it all depends on how long the party goes on.

> *Yours,*
> *Manella."*

She deliberately did not put the letter in an envelope so that Mrs. Bell could read it.

With the money in her pocket and the pistol, she slipped upstairs to her bed-room.

She reckoned this would give her at least two, if not three days, in which to disappear.

By then she must make it impossible for her Uncle to find her.

At the same time, as she crept down the stairs with *Flash* at her side, she felt frightened.

She had always lived in this house where she was born, with her Father and Mother to protect her.

Now she was going out into a strange world of which she knew nothing.

If she had to come back ignominiously, she would be confronted not only by her Uncle's anger, but also by marriage to the Duke.

'I have to be successful . . I have to!' she thought as she went out through a side door towards the stables.

She knew that Glover would not be about at this time of the morning, and the only help he had in the stables was his son of sixteen.

He would be with him in his cottage.

There was however a new groom whom her Uncle had brought with him from London.

She had only just had a glimpse of him and thought he looked a rather unprepossessing man.

She had no trouble to find out where he slept.

It could be in the stables, or inside the house.

She wondered if he was aware that her Uncle intended to sell *Heron*.

If he did, he might make a scene about her taking the horse away.

Everything was quiet in the yard.

When she entered the stable itself, there was only the sound of the horses moving in their stalls.

She glanced at the room at the end where the stable-boys used to sleep in the past.

To her relief it was empty.

This meant that her Uncle's groom had been accommodated in the house.

Hastily, because she was afraid that somebody might appear, she saddled *Heron* and tied her bundle to the back of his saddle.

Then she opened the stable-door.

She felt as if the sounds of his hoofs on the cobbles was alarmingly loud.

Then she knew it was only because she was afraid she would be prevented from leaving at the very last minute.

The sky was now brighter than when she had left the house.

The stars were beginning to fade as the dawn broke.

She took *Heron* to the mounting-block.

Climbing on to it, she seated herself on the saddle.

She moved off, not going through the arch which led to the front of the house, but out the back way.

Once they were in the open, Manella let *Heron* break into a trot.

At the same time, she checked him from even cantering.

She knew she must get as far away as possible, and did not want him to get tired at the very beginning.

She also had to think of *Flash*.

He was delighted to be going out and was running ahead, looking under hedgerows for rabbits.

He was making it obvious that for him this was a new and exciting adventure.

Manella wished that she felt equally elated.

One part of her brain told her that she was doing the right thing.

But her heart grieved at leaving her home which was full of memories of her Mother and Father.

While she was there, she had always felt they were looking after her as they had when she was a child.

Now she was grown up, on her own, and facing a strange and frightening world all by herself.

She rode Westwards, knowing that in that direction there was undulating country in which there were few houses and no one to notice her.

She had the feeling, although she might be wrong, that her Uncle, once he realised she had run away, would think she had gone southwards.

Since London lay to the North, he would assume that she would avoid the City at all costs.

She rode until the sun came out, and as it grew hotter she tried to keep in the shade of trees.

After about three hours it was obvious that *Heron* was not as sprightly as he had been when they started.

He was quite content to go at a gentle trot.

Flash too had ceased running ahead and quietly padded along behind.

Manella saw hardly anybody, riding from field to field, rather than moving along any of the lanes.

This would have meant eventually passing through villages.

Manella was well aware of how curious villagers could be.

A stranger always aroused comment, especially one who was riding a fine horse.

With *Flash* at her heels, it would be certain that anyone who saw her would take notice.

They would remember later that they had seen her pass.

On and on they went until she realised it must be nearly noon and she was feeling hungry.

Too late, she thought it was very foolish of her to have come away without any food.

She had stopped twice already to let *Heron* and *Flash* drink from a clear stream.

At the last stop she had dismounted to hold her hands in the water and also to splash it onto her face.

It was very hot, and getting hotter.

She began to think she would be wise to rest.

At the same time, she was anxious to put as great a distance as was possible between herself and her Uncle.

She reckoned that by now she had been riding for over seven hours.

That meant she was no longer in a neighbourhood where anyone was likely to recognise her.

"I am safe . . I am sure I am safe!" she told herself reassuringly.

She thought however that it would be a mistake to eat at an Inn where she would undoubtedly be asked questions.

The best thing would be to find a village-shop where she could perhaps purchase some slices of ham.

Accordingly, a mile or so further on she left the fields for a lane, moving along it slowly.

As she expected, she soon saw ahead the roofs of some thatched cottages and the spire of a Church.

As she drew nearer, it all looked very quiet and peaceful.

The cottages had gardens in front of them which were bright with flowers.

The doors and the windows were well painted and in good repair.

She was not surprised a minute or two later to see the bow-window of what looked like a prosperous village-shop.

There was no one about in the street, except for a few children playing with a ball.

There was also a dog with them, who slouched away at the sight of *Flash*.

Manella rode up to the shop and dismounted.

She attached *Heron*'s reins to a large wooden stump which had obviously been used before to tether horses.

With *Flash* at her heels, she walked into the shop.

She had been right in thinking it was prosperous, for she saw at a glance there were a great many full shelves.

There was freshly baked bread on the counter, and a ham that had recently been carved on a table behind it.

As she entered, a middle-aged man wearing spectacles and with a pleasant face rose from a chair in which he had been sitting.

"G'marnin', Ma'am," he greeted her, "an' wot can Oi do fer ye?"

"I would like two slices of your ham which I am sure is delicious," Manella answered, "and I was wondering if you, or perhaps there is a Butcher in the village, could give me some scraps of meat for my dog?"

The Shop-keeper peered over the counter at *Flash*.

"That be a foin-lookin' dog ye has there, Ma'am!" he remarked.

"He is a Setter." Manella replied.

The Shop-keeper nodded as if he remembered that Setters were a special breed of Spaniel.

44

Then he started to sharpen a long, thin knife before he cut the ham.

"What is this village called?" Manella asked.

Before he could reply the door through which she had entered was flung open.

A man who looked like a Senior Servant came bursting in.

"Mr. Getty! Mr. Getty!" he cried. "There's a disaster up at t'Castle, an' you're the only one as can help us!"

The Shop-keeper put down his knife.

"A disaster, Mr. Dobbins?" he asked. "What can 'ave occurred?"

"It's Mrs. Wade," Mr. Dobbins replied. "She's 'ad a stroke! She's paralysed!"

"I don't believe it!" Mr. Getty exclaimed. "How can it 'ave 'appened?"

"She's bin complainin' of not feeling well," Mr. Dobbins replied, "I 'spect it's worry over wot to cook for 'Is Lordship. It's been too much for 'er."

Mr. Getty shook his head.

"She be gettin' on in years. I've told 'er often 'nough she should retire."

"She were that excited when she 'eard 'Is Lordship were arrivin' today," Mr. Dobbins said. "I sent for the Doctor, but I knows even before 'e tell us so, there be nothin' we can do for 'er."

"Oi'm right sorry," Mr. Getty murmured.

"Well, what I've come for," Mr. Dobbins said in a different voice, "is to ask 'e if you knows of anyone as can take Mrs. Wade's place, at least while we looks round for someone else."

"Take 'er place?" Mr. Getty asked. "D'you mean – do th' cookin'?"

"'Course that's wot I means," Mr. Dobbins replied. "With 'Is Lordship arrivin' with three friends this evenin' and talk o' more people coming on Saturday."

Mr. Getty threw up his hands.

"That be enough for anyone t'cope with, an' well I knows, Mr. Dobbins, there be nobody as can cook as well as Mrs. Wade."

"That be the truth an' no one can say different," Mr. Dobbins agreed. "But we can't 'ave 'Is Lordship sittin' down to an empty table! There must be someone in th' village you can suggest?"

Mr. Getty made a helpless gesture with his hands.

Then as the two men stood looking at each other, Manella said without really thinking:

"I can cook!"

If the roof had fallen in the two men could not have been more surprised.

"Ye can cook, Ma'am? Ye say ye can cook?" Mr. Getty asked as if he did not believe her.

"Very well, as it happens," Manella answered. "In fact I had intended to ask you if there was anywhere I could find employment in this charming village."

For a moment there was complete silence as both men continued to look at her.

Then Mr. Dobbins said in a somewhat pompous manner:

46

"I think I should explain that 'Is Lordship expects a very high standard of cooking. Mrs. Wade were only saying yesterday that, 'avin' been in France for so long, 'e'd be expecting some French dishes as is not often seen in England."

"I am French by birth," Manella said, "and I have been able to cook French dishes of the sort I expect you require since I was a child."

Mr. Getty put his hand up to his forehead.

"It certainly seems as if you've struck lucky, Mr. Dobbins," he said. "Who'd a thought that a Lady as was buying two slices o' ham from me could cook in the French fashion?"

Mr. Dobbins wanted reassuring.

"You're quite certain," he said, "that you can cook French dishes, as you say you can? It'd be embarrassing like if 'Is Lordship was served up inferior food when 'e's payin' us a visit for the first time after being so long abroad."

"What is His Lordship's name?" Manella asked.

Mr. Dobbins took a deep breath.

"He be the Marquis o' Buckingdon," he replied, "and that's where you are at the moment, in the village of Buckingdon, which o' course belongs to 'Is Lordship."

Manella's eyes widened.

She had heard of the Marquis of Buckingdon.

Who had not?

After the war the Duke of Wellington had, as might be expected, publicly praised all those who had served under him.

He had specially mentioned the Earl of Buckingdon who had commanded one of his Regiments.

It had been spectacularly successful.

By brilliant tactics the Earl had saved the lives of many men who otherwise would have perished at the hands of the enemy.

Later, when the period of the occupation had ended, the Prince Regent had given a special party for the Earl.

The highlight of the evening was when His Royal Highness had made him a Marquis.

The reason why Manella had been interested in the reports of this in the newspaper was that her Father had often spoken of the Marquis's Father.

They had been at Eton together, and only lost touch when her Father had no longer been able to afford to go to London.

He had also stopped attending Shooting Parties at which the 10th Earl of Buckingdon would undoubtedly have been a guest.

When the Earl died, her Father had sent a wreath.

She remembered too that when Napoleon was finally defeated, it was the 11th Earl of Buckingdon who had been Wellington's 'Right-Hand Man' with the Army of Occupation.

At one time there had seemed to be hardly a day when he was not mentioned in *The Morning Post*.

That was the only newspaper her Father bought.

Then when the Occupation finally came to an end, there were no further eulogies about the new Marquis.

He was then only mentioned in the *Court Circular*, which was by no means so interesting.

Manella thought it might be exciting to cook for the man who had stood out as a hero among his contemporaries.

She therefore said quickly:

"I have heard of His Lordship, and I promise you he will not be disappointed in my cooking, even though he has spent several years in France."

"There you are, Mr. Dobbins," Mr. Getty said. "No one can say fairer than that. If you ask me, you was born under a lucky star, finding someone as can cook just at the moment when you needs it."

"I agree with you." Mr. Dobbins replied.

He turned to Manella.

"Are you prepared . . Miss, . . to come up to th' Castle wi' me right away?"

He hesitated before he addressed her as 'Miss'.

Manella saw him glance at her hand to see if she was wearing a wedding-ring.

She was just about to acquiesce and say she would go with him, when *Flash* moved beside her.

"There is one condition I must make, Mr. Dobbins," she said, "and that is if I come and cook for the Marquis, I can bring with me my horse and my dog."

She thought there was a look of incredulity on Mr. Dobbin's face.

Then, because he was so desperate, he said:

"Of course! That'll be all right! There's plenty of room in th' stables at th' Castle."

49

Manella smiled.

"Then I will gladly come," she said.

She held out her hand to Mr. Getty.

"It has been a pleasure to meet you," she said, "and although I will not now require your delicious ham, perhaps I can come for some another day."

"You'll be very welcome, Miss," Mr. Getty said with a smile.

Mr. Dobbins opened the door and Manella stepped out into the sunshine.

As she walked towards *Heron* he followed her.

"That be a fine 'orse you 'ave there, Miss," he said admiringly, "very fine!"

"Thank you," Manella replied.

She was aware that there was a note of curiosity in his voice.

It was obvious he was wondering why, with a horse like that, she should be looking for employment.

Then unexpectedly he said:

"Will you tell me your name? I, as you know, am Mr. Dobbins, and I'm Butler to 'Is Lordship."

It was what Manella had expected and she wondered what she should reply.

Then she told herself that if her Uncle was making enquiries as to where she was, he would not expect that she would have described herself as French.

The first French name that came into her head was her Grandmother's.

"My name, Mr. Dobbins," she said slowly, "is Chenon. It is of course French, and although I have

50

lived all my life in England, my parents came over just before the Revolution."

She felt quite safe in saying that because a great number of *émigrés* had fled from France.

It would explain how she knew so much about French cooking.

Mr. Dobbins thought for a moment.

Then he said:

"If you'll excuse me sayin' so, you looks too young to be a Cook, and too young to have anything to do with the Revolution. It'd be best therefore to introduce you to the Household as Miss Chinon an' not go into details as to 'ow you can cook in the French fashion."

He mispronounced the name.

It was also obvious he thought that for the Marquis to have a Cook who was really French could be embarrassing.

She smiled at him and said:

"I am delighted to be called Miss Chinon, and thank you, Mr. Dobbins, for being kind enough to employ me."

Mr. Dobbins had driven from the Castle in a small cart drawn by a well-bred horse.

It was standing not far from *Heron* and was obviously well-trained.

Despite the fact that it was not secured it had made no effort to move away.

Mr. Dobbins climbed into the cart saying:

"Follow me, Miss Chinon."

Manella managed to climb up into *Heron*'s saddle.

As she rode after Mr. Dobbin's cart she waved to Mr. Getty who was watching them go.

She was not surprised to find that along one side of the road there was a high wall which obviously enclosed the grounds of the Castle.

They had not gone very far before they came to some imposing wrought-iron gates tipped with gold and flanked on either side by a lodge.

The Butler drove his cart through the entrance and Manella followed him down an avenue of oak-trees.

As she did so she thought she had been extraordinarily lucky.

If nothing else, she at least had a bed for the night for herself and a stable for *Heron*.

She only hoped she would not disappoint the Marquis or Mr. Dobbins, who had trusted her when she told him she could cook.

It was her Grandmother who had taught her French cooking.

"When I was a girl," the Countess had said, "my Mother insisted on my learning all the most delicious and traditional French dishes to please my Father."

She smiled before she went on:

"When I married your Grandfather, he used to ask me sometimes to cook him one of my special French dishes which no English Cook could manage, however hard they tried."

"What is the secret, Grandmama?" Manella had asked.

"That is what I am going to teach you," her Grandmother promised.

Manella found it fascinating to create dishes which were so very different from English fare, as provided by Mrs. Bell.

Sometimes, when her Father had been away for the night, or even just for a day, her Mother would say:

"Let us give Papa a treat, Dearest, and cook him something special to show that we are glad to have him home again."

Like conspirators they would hurry down to the Kitchen.

Because her Grandmother had taught her so well, both her Mother and Mrs. Bell would watch her.

They were fascinated as she prepared one or two French dishes that were so different from what they usually ate.

Manella told herself now that she had never imagined for a moment that she would ever become a professional Cook.

As if Fate was taking a hand in her destiny, the position had been there waiting for her when she least expected it.

As she rounded the drive the Castle came in sight.

It was just the sort of house, she thought, in which the Marquis with all his Honours should live.

It was very large and the great town of the original Castle was still standing.

Manella was to learn later that it had been built after the Battle of Agincourt.

In the previous century the remains of the Castle had been converted and added to in order to create an enormous Palladian house.

From a tall centre block jutted out an East and a West wing.

The East wing connected with the Old Castle.

The house now had over a hundred windows glittering in the sunshine.

The court-yard in front of it sloped down to a lake which was spanned by an ancient bridge.

The gardens around the house were ablaze with flowers.

Behind the castle stood trees on rising ground which made a spectacular background, like a setting for a precious jewel.

In fact the house was so lovely that Manella felt she must be imagining it and at any moment it would disappear.

"I am so lucky!" she told herself again.

She bent forward to pat *Heron*'s neck.

"And you are lucky too, " she said. "I am quite certain that if the Marquis lives in such comfort and luxury, your stable will be comfortable too."

As they passed over the bridge, Manella found herself saying a little prayer of thanks.

"Thank You, God, . . thank, . . You!" she said. "I am sure Uncle Herbert will never find me here!"

CHAPTER THREE

When Mr. Dobbins and Manella arrived at the
Castle, they entered through the front door.

This, Manella thought, was a concession because
the Marquis was not at home and she was new.

She was tremendously impressed with the marble
hall with its Greek statues standing in alcoves.

There was also a magnificent marble mantelpiece.

The staircase had alternating gold and crystal
stair-rails, and it curved upwards towards an exquisitely painted ceiling.

Manella had left *Heron* with a groom, but *Flash*
had followed her into the house.

The Butler glanced at him before he said:

"I'll find the Housekeeper, Miss Chinon, an'I
suppose your dog has always lived in the house with
you?"

"Yes, he has!" Manella said firmly. "And he
sleeps by my bed."

She thought Mr. Dobbins looked slightly apprehensive.

He went ahead of her up the stairs.

As they reached the landing, Manella saw coming down the corridor a very impressive figure.

It was the Housekeeper, in rustling black silk with a huge silver chatelaine at her waist.

"Good afternoon, Mrs. Franklin," the Butler said. "I've brought you a new Cook!"

"A new Cook?" the elderly Housekeeper exclaimed in astonishment.

She was looking at Manella as she spoke and said before Mr. Dobbins could speak:

"Surely, you don't mean this young lady?"

"I do indeed!" Mr. Dobbins affirmed. "And she's assured me and Mr. Getty that she's a very good Cook – in fact she's specially proficient in French dishes!"

Mrs. Franklin looked doubtful.

"I promise you," Manella said in a quiet voice, "that I really am a good Cook, and I am confident His Lordship will be satisfied."

"If that is so, we're very lucky!" Mrs. Franklin said.

At the same time she was obviously sceptical that this strange and far too pretty young woman was speaking the truth.

"Now what we've to find, Mrs. Franklin," Mr. Dobbins said briskly, "is a room where Miss Chinon can have her dog with her."

"Her dog?" Mrs. Franklin exlaimed. "We never allow the Staff to have pets of their own."

There was an uncomfortable pause until Manella said quietly:

"*Flash* has been with me ever since he was a puppy. He is perfectly house-trained and as I have explained to Mr. Dobbins, I cannot stay and cook for you unless I can have both my horse and my dog with me."

Manella saw Mr. Dobbins look at Mrs. Franklin frantically and realised she was acquiescing.

"Very well, Miss Chinon," she said. "If you'll come with me, I'll find you a room."

It was then Manella remembered that she had left her clothes on her saddle.

"I am sorry, Mr. Dobbins," she said, "but would you be very kind and send someone to fetch the bundle which is attached to my saddle? There are also some shoes in the pockets."

"I'll do that, Miss Chinon," Mr. Dobbins said, "and thank you. Thank you very much for helping us out of our difficulties."

He gave Mrs. Franklin a sharp look.

He obviously was warning her not to upset Miss Chinon, since otherwise they would find themselves without a Cook.

As he went down the stairs Mrs. Franklin, realising that Mr. Dobbins was right, said in a different tone of voice:

"I think it would be wise, Miss Chinon, not to put you with the other Staff at the top of the house as you've got a dog with you. It might give them ideas, and I have a horror of having to tolerate someone's cat or, as one housemaid wished to bring with her, a white rabbit."

Manella laughed.

"I can understand, Mrs. Franklin, that you have no wish to have a Menagerie in this beautiful house. At the same time, I cannot be separated from my dog."

"His late Lordship, God rest his soul, felt the same," the Housekeeper said. "His Spaniels went everywhere with him."

"You must be very proud of the Marquis," Manella said. "Although I come from a different part of the country altogether, I have read about his bravery in the war and what His Royal Highness the Prince Regent said about him when he gave him his Marquisate."

"We're indeed proud of His Lordship," Mrs. Franklin agreed. "And he were the nicest little boy as ever was."

She walked on down the corridor until she opened the last door.

"This is a room that's seldom used," she said, "except when we're so full that all the larger rooms on this floor are in use."

It was a pleasant enough bed-room, Manella thought, but obviously intended for a bachelor.

There was no dressing-table – just a mirror over the chest-of-drawers.

The oak wardrobe had a masculine look about it.

There was what appeared to be a comfortable bed and a large window which overlooked the front of the house and the lake.

"This will suit me perfectly," Manella said, "and thank you for being so *understanding*."

She emphasised the word and Mrs. Franklin knew she was referring to *Flash*.

"Now if there's anything you want – ask me," she said. "For the moment, however, I'm sure you want to see the Kitchen, as there's really very little time to make preparations before His Lordship's arrival."

Manella took off the small hat she was wearing and put it down on a chair.

Pushing her golden hair into place she said:

"I am quite ready, and of course I realise there is a lot of work ahead of me."

Mrs. Franklin took her down a side-staircase to the Ground Floor.

They passed the Pantry, which she could see was quite large.

She knew it was where a footman would sleep in order to guard the safe.

Mrs. Franklin, who was moving ahead, opened a door into the Kitchen.

It was, as Manella had expected, a large room with a high ceiling, and there were beams with hooks on which to hang food.

It was something she could remember seeing when she was no more than a child.

There was a ham, several ducks, a number of pigeons, and some onions tied together by their stalks.

She walked towards the huge stove where standing

beside it stirring something in a saucepan was a girl of about sixteen.

Another girl of the same age was shelling peas.

They looked up at her in surprise.

"Bessie and Jane will help you, Miss Chinon," Mrs. Franklin said. "I'm afraid they're very young, but Mrs. Wade was teaching them to do things the way she liked, and found the older women we had previously were too slow."

"I am sure they will be a great help," Manella said smiling at them.

The two girls smiled back shyly.

"I don't know what they've prepared for luncheon," Mrs. Franklin said, "but I suggested before Mrs. Wade was took ill that as there'd be so much to cook for tonight, we'd best have something cold."

"I think that is a very good idea," Manella said. "And I can see there is a ham, at any rate."

She pointed up to the beam from which the ham was suspended.

"There should be a good deal more than that," Mrs. Franklin replied. "What's happened to the chicken you was cooking yesterday, Bessie?"

"It be in t'Larder, Mrs. Franklin," Bessie replied.

"Then run and fetch it, child, fetch it!" Mrs. Franklin ordered. "And anything else that Miss Chinon can give us."

As Bessie hurried away, Manella remembered what her home had been like when her Mother was alive.

"I suppose," she said, "you and Mr. Dobbins have

60

your luncheon in the Housekeeper's Room, Mrs. Franklin? And the Kitchen Staff and the housemaids and footmen eat in the Servants' Hall."

"That's right," Mrs. Franklin agreed.

She spoke with an expression of approval in her eyes.

She accepted now that Manella knew how a Gentleman's household was organised.

"And you, of course," Mrs. Franklin added, "will have your meals with Mr. Dobbins and me."

"I am sure the girls will have prepared some vegetables," Manella said, "and I will have luncheon sent to the Housekeeper's Room as quickly as possible."

"That's very helpful of you, Miss Chinon," Mrs. Franklin replied.

She swept out of the Kitchen with a rustle of her silk gown.

When she had gone, Manella smiled at the two girls.

Bessie had just come back carrying a tray with the cold chicken on one plate and a large sirloin of beef on another.

"Personally I am hungry!" Manella said. "While I finish off the vegetables which you have been cooking, I should be very grateful if you Bessie would cut me a slice of chicken and if Jane will get down that ham which is hanging overhead."

The girls hurried to obey her and she ate some chicken as she put the vegetables into china dishes.

She also gave several small pieces to *Flash*.

She was thinking that, however busy she might be, she must go to the stables to see that *Heron* was all right.

She was sure there would be water in his stall and a good feed of oats.

She could not believe that the Marquis, of all people, would skimp on his horses.

What mattered at the moment more than anything else was that neither *Heron* nor *Flash* should go hungry.

. . . .

By the time the afternoon was drawing to a close Manella had everything prepared for dinner.

She had not been so foolish as to start by making French dishes the moment she arrived.

She had to have the right ingredients, for one thing, and, for another, to get to know her way round the Kitchen.

She did not go to the Housekeeper's Room to have her luncheon.

Instead she ate in the Kitchen alone after the girls had gone to the Servants' Hall.

Manella learnt that there were six footmen, five under-housemaids, and the two girls in the Kitchen to feed.

There was also one old man who she gathered brought in the coal and the wood for the fires.

She had sent a message to Mrs. Franklin knowing that the Butler and the Housekeeper would understand that she had too much to do to join them.

She had just finished her luncheon and was thinking the cold chicken and a home-cured ham were delicious because she was so hungry.

It was then that Mr. Dobbins came in to join her.

"I forgot to tell you, Miss Chinon", he said as he came into the Kitchen, "that Mrs. Wade had prepared her dinner for tonight, and the menu has been written out by 'Is Lordship's Secretary."

"That is what the girls have told me," Manella replied, "and I therefore intend tonight to serve exactly what Mrs. Wade had planned."

She thought Mr. Dobbins gave a sigh of relief.

He must have thought it would be difficult in those circumstances for her to go wrong.

He then said:

"In the excitement of bringing you back in triumph, Miss Chinon, I also forgot that you should have seen Mr. Watson, 'Is Lordship's Secretary, before you started work. He would like to talk to you now, and to discuss your salary."

"Thank you," Manella said, "and perhaps you would show me the way."

She was taken by Mr. Dobbins through what she thought was a labyrinth of passages. Eventually they came to the Secretary's Room on the other side of the house.

Mr. Watson was an elderly man who she learnt subsequently had been at the Castle with the Marquis's Father ever since he had inherited.

When she was introduced to him by Mr. Dobbins, he stared at her in astonishment.

Then he said:

"You are really a Cook, Miss Chinon?"

"I really am," Manella said, "and I know you are being polite in not adding that I look too young."

"It had certainly crossed my mind," Mr. Watson admitted.

"I do not think you will be disappointed," she said. "But of course, if you are, I need only stay until you find another Cook."

"I feel sure that is something I will not have to do," Mr. Watson said gallantly.

Mr. Dobbins withdrew and Manella sat down in a chair opposite the desk.

"Now I have to ask you what wages you are asking, and I appreciate, Miss Chinon, that you have saved us from being in a very uncomfortable situation, at what, I might say, was 'the eleventh hour'."

Manella laughed.

"If you are suggesting I am going to blackmail you, I will not do that, Mr. Watson. I will accept very gratefully whatever you consider is a fair wage."

Mr. Watson somewhat tentatively told her what Mrs. Wade was receiving.

Manella accepted it without further discussion.

She thought if she stayed only a few weeks, it would give her enough money to proceed on her way without being afraid that *Heron* and *Flash* would go hungry.

When she rose from her chair she held out her hand to Mr. Watson.

"Thank you very much," she said. "*You* may be

grateful that I have appeared unexpectedly when you were in difficulty, but *I* also am grateful to you because I was looking for a position, and was not quite sure how quickly I would find one."

"I can only hope, Miss Chinon, that you will be happy here," Mr. Watson said.

Manella hurried back to the Kitchen.

She thought everything was going well.

The only difficulty now would be if the Marquis disapproved of her.

Then she told herself that she was very unlikely to come into direct contact with him.

Any comment he had to make about her cooking would be conveyed to her by the Butler.

She then started to work hard to get everything ready for the dinner.

There were to be five courses, starting with soup and ending with a savoury.

Manella knew all the recipes very well.

The planned menu was what Mrs. Bell had always considered the 'right food' for presenting.

She was an excellent Cook in that everything tasted exactly as it should. She had not however been particularly imaginative.

Sometimes Manella had longed for the delicious French dishes her Grandmother had taught her to make.

Then she would go into the Kitchen and say to Mrs. Bell:

"I have nothing much to do today, so I have come to help you."

"You don't deceive me with that honeyed talk, M'Lady," Mrs. Bell would reply sharply. "You're after makin' that 'Froggy' food! You should be ashamed to eat it when that wicked man has killed so many of our kith and kin!"

It was something she always said.

At the same time, she would let Manella make *Crêpes Suzettes*, or a *Strawberry Sorbet*, and even commended her on how delicious it was when she had done so.

"Tomorrow night," Manella told herself, "I will give His Lordship a treat."

Manella cooked the English menu perfectly, just as Mrs. Bell would have done.

It was taken into the Dining-Room by Mr. Dobbins and his footmen.

Mr. Dobbins came back smiling.

"'Is Lordship's enjoying himself," he said, "an so's the Lady he's brought with him."

"Lady?" Manella enquired.

"That's right," Mr. Dobbins said, "and 'er's a Frenchy, believe it or not, just like you!"

"What is her name?" Manella enquired.

"Her be the *Comtesse* d'Orbrey," Mr. Dobbins pronounced her name rather strangely, "and 'e calls her Yvette."

Manella was surprised that the Marquis would entertain anyone French.

Then she thought he had doubtless met her when he was with the Army of Occupation.

"And who are the men?" she enquired.

"One calls 'imself a *Comte*, and 'e seems to be 'er brother," Mr. Dobbins replied. "'Is name's a bit queer, de Fuisse, I think it is, and the other be just a *Monsieur*."

"And again French?" asked Manella.

"From Paris 'e said 'e was," Mr. Dobbins answered. "An ugly-looking man, but he seems to amuse 'Is Lordship."

"Well, as long as they are satisfied with the dinner, that is all that matters," Manella said.

"They certainly eats it!" Mr. Dobbins assured her. "And sucking up, they were, to 'Is Lordship. 'Anging on every word 'e said, 'specially th' *Comtesse*."

Manella was not particulary interested in the Marquis's guests.

She was wondering if she would get a chance to see him.

Then she reminded herself that her bed-room window looked out over the front of the house.

If by no other way, she would see him mounting a horse outside the front door, or perhaps driving a Phaeton.

She was by this time very tired.

She had hardly slept at all the night before, worrying how she could get away from her Uncle.

As soon as the Kitchen was tidy, she sent the girls to bed.

She was determined to follow them as soon as possible.

She had however to put *Flash* out first and she took him out by the back door.

'Tomorrow,' she thought, 'I must explore the Castle and find out where everything is. But for the moment, I must just be content to know I have a comfortable bed to sleep in, which I do not have to pay for.'

There were some bushes near the back door.

Between them there was a path lined with shrubs.

As the moon was rising in the sky it was easy to see.

She walked along the path and found that it led to the stables.

She knew then that she could not possibly go to bed without seeing *Heron*.

There was a long row of doors and she opened the first one.

By the light on the wall she could see to her delight that the stalls were roomy and comfortable.

She passed a number of horses before she eventually came to where *Heron* was stabled.

Going into his stall she put her arms round his neck and he nuzzled against her.

"We are safe, my Darling," she said. "We are here, and I do not believe Uncle Herbert or anyone else could guess where I am."

She felt as if *Heron*, whom she had always talked to, understood what she was saying.

She patted him and made a fuss of him, and saw that his manger was full of the most expensive oats.

There was also a bucket of fresh water for him to drink.

She went back to the house followed by *Flash*.

The Kitchen was in darkness and the only sound was coming from the Pantry.

She slipped past without being noticed, and went up the side-stairs to the First Floor.

The guests, she knew, would all be occupying the State Rooms which she had not yet seen.

They were all further along the corridor.

When she went into her own room it seemed like a haven of peace.

She knew that for tonight at any rate she would be able to sleep without being afraid.

Flash made himself at home by settling down comfortably beside the bed.

As Manella undressed and patted him before she said her prayers, she told herself that she was very lucky.

. . . .

The following morning Manella awoke with a start.

When she looked at the clock on the Mantelpiece however, she found it was not yet six o'clock.

It was a relief because she had forgotten to tell the girls to call her and was afraid she might have overslept.

She hurried downstairs to prepare the breakfast.

She was informed that His Lordship required breakfast at eight o'clock.

"'E's goin' ridin'," a footman told her, "but tomorrer 'e'll ride early an' 'ave 'is breakfast after."

"Well, as long as I am warned, I can have everything ready," Manella answered.

She was thinking as she cooked that she must somehow find time to exercise *Heron*.

She felt it would be a good thing for him to have a quiet day to-day, having been ridden so far yesterday.

But he was young and spirited.

He would soon grow restless if she did not ride him as she always did.

'But if the Marquis rides early,' she calculated, 'I shall have to go out earlier still, or else slip away in the afternoon.'

She felt sure that once luncheon was over the servants expected to take it easy until tea-time.

If she prepared the sandwiches and baked the cakes beforehand, they would be ready to be taken from the Kitchen into the Drawing-Room.

"I have to plan my work properly," Manella told herself severely. "It would be a great mistake to overlook something I ought to do the moment I have arrived."

She therefore concentrated on the breakfast, making six different dishes for the Dining-Room.

She put the eggs, fish, mushrooms and kidneys that Mrs. Wade had left ready into silver serving-dishes.

They were kept hot by means of lighted candles underneath them.

At the last moment, she realized she had forgotten

last night to put a loaf of bread into the oven so that it would be ready for the morning.

"They will have to manage with toast," she told herself, "but it is something I must not forget again."

She could have blamed the girls for not reminding her.

But she knew they themselves had not been at the Castle for very long.

Naturally they could not be expected to know how people like the Marquis's friends expected things to be done.

'I must remember exactly how we used to do it at home.' Manella told herself.

The past started to come back to her mind.

It made her realise how much things at home had deteriorated after her mother's death.

As, thanks to Uncle Herbert, they became poorer and poorer, one luxury after another had disappeared and was eventually forgotten.

While she was getting the luncheon, she started to think of what she would give the Marquis for dinner that evening.

It was exciting to think that she could make the French dishes her Grandmother had taught her without worrying about the expense.

She could now choose the ingredients that had been set aside at home as being too extravagant.

Finally she had her menu prepared.

When the game-keepers and the gardeners came in for her orders she told them exactly what they had to find.

"We'll do us best, Miss," they said scratching their heads, "bu' it b'aint be easy."

"I know," Manella smiled. "But none of us can do enough for His Lordship, can we?"

It was exactly the right note to strike.

They all agreed that 'the Marquis deserved the best', and no mistake.

By tea-time, Manella had everything prepared.

When she learnt that the Marquis and his friends were sitting comfortably in the Drawing-Room, she thought she might explore a little more of the Castle.

She had also learnt that more of the Marquis's friends were arriving the next day.

The housemaids had been told that eight more bed-rooms were to be made ready.

The grooms were expecting three or four carriages and had to see to the stabling.

The housemaids were preparing for the new guests and the servants they would bring with them.

Manella thought she could now safely slip away.

She had decided to go first to the Music-Room, and thought after that she would go to the Library and the Ball-Room.

She had eaten luncheon with Mrs. Franklin in the Housekeeper's Room and she had learnt how much there was to see.

"I expect you'll enjoy the pictures in the Gallery," the Head-housemaid said. "And when you're lookin' at 'em, remember it's us as 'as to keep the floor polished, an' that's a task, I can tell ye!"

The Curator, who was an old man and who had

also lunched with them, told Manella he would show her the books in the Library.

Some, he said, were First Editions and very valuable.

She thought it was unusual for a Curator to have his meals in the Housekeeper's Room, but he said he felt lonely and enjoyed a chat.

Mr. Watson, he said, was unfortunately only interested in Mathematics and finance!

Manella had laughed.

Yet she understood why Mr. Watson had his meals taken to him on a tray by one of the footmen.

That was another item she had to prepare.

Because she felt sorry for him, she tried to make his dishes look as appetising as possible.

She therefore decorated them in a way that was certainly more French than English.

She decided not to visit the Library yet, because she knew the Curator would want to keep her talking to him.

Then there would be no time to see the rest of the rooms she wanted to visit.

She therefore went first to the Music-Room, which was fascinating.

There were murals on the walls and a very impressive ceiling.

The Ball-Room, which had not been used since before the war, was awe-inspiring.

With the chandeliers lit and the room filled with flowers, it could be the most romantic room she had ever seen.

She had been told there was no one in the East Wing.

She was wondering whether she had time to explore that part of the Castle.

Then she decided she must leave it for another day.

She however looked at the huge oak door which separated it from the newer part of the Castle.

As she did so she became aware of another door and because she was curious she opened it.

She found it led to a Chapel.

Because it was situated between the ancient door and the new building she guessed it was as old as the original Castle.

It was certainly very lovely, with stained-glass windows and carved pews that were obviously hundreds of years old.

There was a cloth over the altar, but no flowers had been arranged on either side of the Cross, which was gold and set with precious stones.

Manella was aware of an atmosphere of sanctity in the Chapel. It must have come she thought from the prayers of those who had worshipped there for many generations.

She knelt down at the altar rail.

She was just saying a prayer of thankfulness that she was for the moment safe, when she heard voices.

She felt they were coming nearer to the Chapel and looked round.

She had no wish to be discovered by the Marquis or his friends.

She did not want to have to explain her position in the household.

On one side of the altar was a door which she guessed would lead into a Vestry.

Quickly she moved towards it, and going in found she was right.

It was a very small Vestry, but there was a surplice hanging on one wall and on the other there was an elaborate vestment.

Manella thought it was what a Parson would wear at Christmas or some other Festival.

There was a table in the centre on which stood two Registers, and several Prayer Books.

She pressed the door almost closed behind her.

As she did so she realised that two men had come into the Chapel and were talking in French.

She was sure they must be the *Comte* de Fiosse, whose name Mr. Dobbins had mispronounced, and the other French gentleman.

"This will do nicely," one Frenchman said.

"I thought you would think so," the other replied. "I have told Father Anton to come in secretly and to hide here until we appear."

"There is no one likely to be looking for him," the first Frenchman replied, "and I ascertained from His Lordship that they have a Service here for the Staff only on Sundays. The Vicar from the village takes it."

"Father Anton will be here as soon as we have finished dinner," the other man said. "The only person we now have to see is the Cook."

"I expect she is some fat old body who has been here since the year 'dot'," was the reply, "and for a couple of *louis* she will do anything!"

"Do not forget to make it sovereigns," the other said.

"Of course I won't," was the answer. "I am not as stupid as that, and I think a 'fiver' would be about right."

"You must make very sure she understands what we want."

"You can trust me to do that," the first Frenchman replied. "I have a way with older women."

"And with young ones!" his friend added.

They both laughed.

Without saying any more they turned and walked from the Chapel.

Manella heard their footsteps going further and further away down the passage.

She then came from her hiding-place in the Vestry.

She found it hard to believe what she had heard.

There was obviously something very sinister taking place.

Why was a Priest necessary? A Catholic Priest from the way they had spoken about him.

"I do not understand," she told herself.

Then she remembered one of the Frenchmen, she expected it was the *Comte*, was going to see the 'Cook'.

He thought she would be an elderly woman.

Manella could not imagine why he wished to see her, but it was obviously something very important.

'Of one thing I am quite certain,' she thought, 'he will have a shock when he sees me!'

It was a worrying thought.

Then she told herself there was nothing she could do about it.

CHAPTER FOUR

Manella had only just got back to the Kitchen when one of the footmen came in to say:

"Th' *Comte* wishes to speak to ye, Miss. He's in th' Writing-Room."

"And where is that?" Manella enquired.

"I'll show ye," the footman replied.

He was a rather good-looking young man and he smiled at her before he went ahead.

They passed the Pantry.

Then going towards the Hall there was a door on the right-hand side of the corridor.

The footman opened it and Manella saw that it was a small, well-furnished Writing-Room with two desks.

One wall was covered with books.

Standing waiting for her was one of the men she had heard speaking in the Chapel.

As the footman shut the door he stared at her in amazement.

"I asked for the Cook," he said in English.

Manella answered him in French.

"I am the Cook, *Monsieur le Comte*," she said.

She smiled.

"I am French by birth, but I have always lived in England."

"This is certainly a surprise," the *Comte* said. "I was expecting an English Cook who had been with the family for years, and whom I could congratulate on the excellent food she gave us last night."

"I think, being French, *Monsieur*, you will enjoy the meal I am preparing for tonight," Manella said.

"You mean you are giving us French dishes?" the *Comte* asked.

"*Oui, Monsieur*, and I shall be very disappointed if you do not enjoy them," Manella answered.

"I will certainly do that," the *Comte* replied, "especially when I think of how charming and attractive their creator is."

Manella realised that, French fashion, he was flirting with her.

She merely stood waiting, hoping he would think she was in a hurry.

"What I wanted to tell you," the *Comte* began, "besides, of course, complimenting you on your cooking last night, is that my friends and I have planned a little surprise for *Monsieur le Marquis*."

Manella inclined her head, but she did not speak.

"What we intend is to inject in him a little of the *joie de vivre, élan* and enthusiasm that you, *Mademoiselle*, will be aware is very French."

He paused.

Then he drew from the pocket of his coat a small box.

It obviously had originally been a snuff-box.

It was enamel, with what Manella suspected was the *Comte's* crest on the lid.

He held it in his hand and looked down at it reflectively.

Then he said:

"In this box is a powdered herb which you, being so young, *Mademoiselle*, may not have heard of. It is grown in the South of France and has just reached Paris. Anyone who takes it feels an ecstasy, as if they were flying up into the sky."

"It sounds very interesting," Manella said, "and you are quite right, *Monsieur*, I have not heard of it."

"Then you will see its effect this evening," the *Comte* said. "What I want you to do is to put a little – a very little – into the food of *Monsieur le Marquis*."

He frowned and then went on:

"I do not know what your menu will be, but I am sure you can choose something, perhaps served towards the end of the meal, which will absorb quite easily just a small teaspoonful of this magical powder."

He opened the box as he spoke, and Manella saw it was full of white powder.

"Now you quite understand that this is only for *Monsieur le Marquis*," the *Comte* said. "On no account must any of it be wasted on me or my friends."

"I understand," Manella said.

The *Comte* looked round vaguely.

"Into what can I put the powder?" he enquired.

Manella reached out and took the box from his hand.

"I will take it, *Monsieur*," she said, "and in case it gets lost or someone tastes it, I will put a teaspoonful into something safe and lock it away in a drawer."

"That is a good idea," the *Comte* said, approvingly.

"It will not take me more than a minute to hurry to the Kitchen and do what I suggested." Manella said.

She thought he was going to expostulate.

But before she had finished speaking she went out of the room, shutting the door behind her.

Carrying the snuff-box, she went to the Kitchen and found there was no one there.

Taking down a cup from where it hung on the dresser she emptied the whole contents of the snuff-box into it.

She locked the cup containing the white powder safely in a drawer.

Then she re-filled the snuff-box with white flour.

It looked very much the same as the powder she had just removed.

Closing the box she hurried back with it to the Writing-Room.

The *Comte* was waiting for her with a frown on his forehead, as if he was anxious.

"You have been very careful?" he said sharply as Manella entered. "You must give *Monsieur le Marquis* only half a teaspoonful or, I might say, the contents of a small coffee-spoon."

"I understand perfectly, *Monsieur*," Manella replied, "and I have only taken exactly that amount."

"You must be very sure that the footmen serve what is for *Monsieur le Marquis* to him and not to any of us. It would be a disaster if the plate went to the wrong person."

"I understand that," Manella answered, "and I promise you, *Monsieur*, there will be no mistakes."

"I know I can trust you," the *Comte* said putting the snuff-box into his pocket without opening it, "and here is something for your trouble with which you can buy a gown to make you look even lovelier than you are at the moment."

He pressed five sovereigns into her hand and she dropped him a curtsy.

"*Merci beaucoup, Monsieur le Comte*," she said, "You are very kind and I am most grateful."

"It would, you understand, be a great mistake," the *Comte* said softly, "for anybody in the house to know of my generosity."

"Of course, *Monsieur*," Manella agreed.

She went to the door and curtsied again before she left him.

She went back to the Kitchen.

She opened the drawer and looked speculatively at the contents of the cup.

She had an idea in her head and the more she thought about it, the better it became.

Manella started to prepare the dinner earlier than would have been necessary.

But with the *Comte*'s interference there was now an addition to what she had already planned.

When she told Mr. Dobbins they were having a French menu, he had said:

"That's somethin' new for us, but 'Is Lordship may 'ave acquired different tastes bein' so long in France."

"That is what I thought, Mr. Dobbins," Manella smiled, "and I want your help to see that everything goes off smoothly."

"I'm only 'ere to oblige!" Mr. Dobbins said jokingly.

Manella made out the menu and took it along to Mr. Watson.

"French dishes?" he enquired. "You would think that His Lordship would be tired of them by now."

"One can never tire of a good thing," Manella replied, "and French food, I assure you, Mr. Watson, is very, very good."

"Well, there were no complaints about last night's dinner," Mr. Watson said. "And I'll not pretend, Miss Chinon, that you were not a 'gift from the gods' when we most needed it."

"*Merci beaucoup, Monsieur*," Manella replied, "and I like being a goddess!"

She heard him laugh as she left the room to hurry back to the Kitchen.

She had chosen a dinner which she had done many times for her Father.

There was a very delicious Duck Pâté to start with.

She served it on individual plates decorated with rosettes made from baby carrots and small beet-roots.

After that came a cup filled with clear, golden soup.

Every mouthful of which, Manella knew, was a delight.

This was followed by a fresh salmon which the game-keeper had brought in that very morning from the river.

At the same time they had provided her with four young chickens.

'*Petits Poussins*', as Manella had described them on the menu.

She had then hesitated and added between the Fish and the Poussins a Pear *Sorbet*.

She added just a touch of champagne and it was to be served in wine-glasses.

Then, she thought with a twinkle in her eyes, there would be something different from what they had eaten last night.

She concentrated on the *poussins*.

．　．　．　．　．　．　．

Dinner was announced by Dobbins at exactly eight o'clock.

It was late by London standards because the Prince Regent usually dined at seven-thirty.

But while the weather was so fine, the Marquis wanted to be out in the grounds as late as possible.

He had been riding during the afternoon a horse he had purchased at Tattersalls two weeks ago.

It was not completely broken in so he enjoyed the age-old battle between man and beast.

They sat down at the table decorated with orchids.

The *Comtesse* put her hand with its long, thin fingers on his arm and said:

"Dearest Buck, it is so delightful to have you to ourselves. I shall be jealous tomorrow when the rest of your party arrives."

"I hope you are not suggesting in a subtle way that I may neglect you," the Marquis replied.

"I would never allow you to do that," the *Comtesse* said with an innuendo behind every word.

The Marquis had met her in Paris, and found her witty, amusing, and completely insatiable in bed.

After the demands and strains of war he had found that Paris, with an elasticity all of its own, had come back to life.

There was every possible amusement for a man who wished to be amused.

It enabled him to forget the carnage, the suffering and the deprivations of so many years.

Yvette had made sure that the Marquis thought more of her than of anything else.

She was always there when he was not actually on duty with his troops, and he would have been inhuman if he had not found that she was very desirable.

She had made sure, as only a sophisticated woman could, that he desired her.

She was a widow.

Her husband had been killed when he was commanding his Regiment at the battle of Leipsig, the year before Napoleon's Abdication and banishment to Elba in 1814.

Yvette had impressed upon the Marquis, over and over again, that she came from a family of the *ancien régime*.

But her husband had had no choice but to fight for the 'Corsican Corporal', once he had seized power.

"If Henri was alive," she said, "he would have been so glad that the English won, and that you, *mon Brave*, had been recognised as a great soldier."

Her brother the *Comte* confirmed everything she said.

He reiterated over and over again how, though they had escaped the guillotine, their estates were all taken from them during the Revolution.

"The rightful place for aristocrats now is England," he said, "and that is where dearest Yvette wishes to live."

When he said this he gave the Marquis a look which expressed better than words what he was hoping would happen.

The Marquis however had been pursued ever since leaving Eton by women who wished to marry him because of his title.

And for the wealth and power he would inherit when his Father died.

When he did in fact become the Earl, he was fighting in Portugal and more concerned with keeping alive than with his estates at home.

He had however not failed to notice that after he became the Marquis of Buckingdon the invitation cards that appeared on his breakfast-table every morning had increased remarkably in number.

It seemed extraordinary for a man who had so much, that he could admit to himself he had never been in love.

He had been intrigued and at times infatuated.

But he had never been in love to the point where he wished to share the rest of his life with any woman.

Yvette had made it only too obvious in Paris that she wanted to become an English Countess. And now, all the more, to become the Marchioness of Buckingdon.

He thought she was now being rather too persistent.

He told himself that when he returned to London he would not see so much of her.

He had talked, and what man would not, when he was abroad of the house he loved and his horses that meant so much to him.

He had therefore thought it polite, if nothing else

to bring Yvette, her brother and the Frenchman who was nearly always with them to visit Buckingdon Castle.

Now he decided that this would be both the first and the last visit they would make.

He was grateful to them, of course he was grateful, for all they had done for him in Paris.

But now that he was back in England, he knew that he must concentrate on his family and make contact with the friends he had known when he was a boy.

Moreover what was known as the 'Beau Monde' was waiting for him in London.

The Prince Regent had made it very clear that he would be a welcome guest any time he wished to visit Carlton House.

Last night, Yvette had been even more demanding than usual.

The Marquis had actually been a little tired after the long drive from London.

He decided that he would buy her a present of emeralds which matched her eyes, and that would be that.

"At least," Yvette was saying in a soft, seductive voice, "we shall have a little time to ourselves tomorrow before your party arrives."

"Of course we shall," the Marquis answered, "and you must tell me what you would like to do. There are still a lot of things I have not shown you, and my horses are waiting for your orders!"

Yvette smiled at him provocatively.

He knew what she wanted did not include horses.

But he was now aware that she really did not fit in the English Countryside.

He would have been wiser to give a party for her at his house in Berkeley Square.

Dobbins and the footmen were placing the pâté in front of the guests.

The Marquis reached out his hand for the menu.

It was in a gold holder which bore his Coat of Arms.

He read it and said to Yvette:

"I see we have a French dinner tonight, and that of course is in your honour. I only hope that as my Cook is English you will not be disappointed."

"How could I be disappointed in anything in this wonderful Castle of yours," Yvette replied, "and as you know well, Buck, it is made for love."

The Marquis tasted the pâté, and instead of replying to Yvette he said:

"This is excellent! I had no idea Mrs. Wade could make a pâté as good as this!"

"I would like to say we had brought it with us," the *Comte* interposed, "but unfortunately I did not think of it."

"If you had, it would have been 'Coals to Newcastle'!" the Marquis replied. "Do you not agree with me Grave?"

The other Frenchman nodded enthusiastically.

Salmon cooked in its own juices followed the soup.

By this time they were all exclaiming they had never tasted better dishes.

The *Sorbet* was a surprise, then Dobbins went to the Marquis's side.

"Cook asks me to tell you, M'Lord," he said, "that it's usual in this part o' the country, when a man returns from war, for him to be given the 'White Dove of Peace' as a special dish."

He took a deep breath and went on:

"Tis s'posed to bring him luck so's he'll not have to fight again. Cook asks that you eats it all yourself, as is traditional, and not share it with anyone!"

The Marquis listened, then he laughed.

"That is a legend I have never heard before," he said. "Of course I will do what Cooks asks, but I see the 'White Dove of Peace' is not on the menu."

"No, M'Lord," Dobbins replied , "but there are 'Baby Pussins' I think she calls 'em, for everyone else."

The Marquis's eyes twinkled, but he did not correct Dobbins's pronunciation.

A footman put the beautifully cooked *Poussins* in front of the other guests.

They had a very special stuffing and a gravy containing fresh mushrooms as well as the usual breadcrumbs.

On a side plate there was for everyone tiny carrots, no bigger than marbles, baby beetroots of about the same size, and minute green peas.

There were new potatoes cooked 'in their jackets' that were merely a mouthful each.

90

The Marquis tasted his 'White Dove of Peace'.

He thought secretly that it was a delicious, very well cooked pigeon.

He certainly could not find fault with it.

In fact it was more tender than any pigeon he had ever eaten before.

There was a silence while everyone ate.

Then suddenly *Monsieur* Grave, who was sitting opposite the Marquis, made a murmur.

He put out his hands as if to support himself, then fell forward, his face falling into his plate.

The Marquis stared at him in astonishment, thinking he must be drunk.

Then before he could say or do anything, Yvette fell backwards in her chair.

Collapsing, she slipped down under the table.

The Marquis pushed back his chair as the *Comte*, with a crash, fell forward, his hand upsetting his glass of champagne as he did so.

Standing, the Marquis stared at his guests, for the moment speechless.

Then as Dobbins came to his side he said:

"What the devil does this mean? Fetch the Cook! It must be something to do with the food."

Dobbins moved across the room to obey him, while the footmen stood waiting for orders.

They were just staring at the guests as the Marquis was doing.

Manella was in fact waiting just outside the Dining-Room.

She had been afraid that the Marquis might eat

one of the *Poussins* rather than the pigeon she had prepared specially for him.

She had peered into the room so that she could save him, if it was necessary.

She had put all the powder that had been in the snuff-box into the stuffing of the Poussins and into the gravy.

Dobbins had no need to speak to her.

As he reached the door she walked past him and up to where the Marquis was still standing at the head of the table.

As she faced him he looked at her in astonishment and exclaimed:

"You are not Mrs. Wade!"

"Mrs. Wade has been suddenly taken ill, and I have replaced her," Manella said quietly.

"Then you are responsible for this?" the Marquis asked indicating his collapsed guests.

"They have consumed a drug that was intended for you," Manella said.

"For *me*?"

"*Monsieur le Comte* gave me five sovereigns to put half a teaspoonful of what is obviously a drug into your food, and in no one else's. But instead I put a very large quantity of the drug into their food." Manella explained.

"I cannot believe it!" the Marquis exclaimed. "Why ever should he do that?"

"I think you will find the explanation in the Chapel," Manella replied.

The Marquis looked at her and she realised he did not understand.

"I overheard them saying that a Priest, I imagine a Roman Catholic one, would be waiting there after dinner."

She saw from the expression in the Marquis's eyes that at last he understood, and it made him very angry.

There was a hard look in his eyes and his lips tightened into a straight line.

Then he said in a controlled voice:

"Then obviously I must thank you for saving me."

"Any of your *English* admirers, and there are a great many of them, My Lord, would have done the same."

She emphasised the word 'English' and knew that the Marquis would take it as a rebuke.

He was thoughtful for a moment.

Then he said:

"We will discuss this later. In the meantime I will get rid of this rabble."

Manella knew she was dismissed.

She dropped him a small curtsy.

Only when she reached the door did she hear him giving sharp orders to Dobbins as if he was on a battlefield.

She tidied the Kitchen, looking sadly at the Raspberry *Soufflé* she had prepared, just in case it was needed.

The *Poussins* however had done their work very competently.

She had read about drugs of various sorts.

She was intelligent enough to realise that the *Comte* had intended to give the Marquis just enough to sap his will-power.

They would then have taken him from the Dining-Room to the Chapel.

He would have acquiesced without any demur to Yvette's demand to be his wife.

They would have been married by the Priest who was waiting for them.

Then there would have been no escape for him.

'But I saved him!' Manella thought triumphantly. 'Now perhaps he will realise that the French are not to be trusted – either in war or in peace!'

She was aware that she was being disloyal to her Grandmother.

At the same time Napoleon had altered the whole social make-up of France.

It was a very different country from what it had been in the past.

The Staff had all had their dinner earlier; in fact at six o'clock, which was the usual time for them.

Manella therefore had nothing to do now except wait for the Marquis to summon her.

She sat down at the kitchen-table and started to read a book.

It was over three-quarters-of-an-hour later that Dobbins came into the Kitchen.

"'Is Lordship wishes to see you in 'is Study, Miss Chinon," he said, "and you've never 'eard such goin's on!"

"What has happened?" Manella asked.

"'Is Lordship's had th' Phaeton that *Monsieur* Grave came in brought round. They was all three put into it. Sound asleep, they was! Couldn't get a peep out of any of them. Their luggage was thrown up behind and the groom was told to take the lot back to London, or as far as he could get!"

Mr. Dobbins gave a laugh.

"He wasn't at all pleased, settin' off at night with them three squeezed in like sardines."

"They had not . . recovered . . consciousness?" Manella asked a little tentatively.

She had really no wish to kill anyone.

"They got no idea what was happening to 'em. But they was alive all right, the *Comte* snoring as if he were a bear at th' zoo!"

"I expect they will have a headache tomorrow," Manella said.

"That's what I thinks too," Mr. Dobbins replied, "and it serves them right! How dare they try to drug 'Is Lordship? I've told you before, an' I'll tell you again, you can never trust them 'Frogs'."

He suddenly realised to whom he was speaking.

"But you're different, Miss," he said, "as we all knows. You seems to me to be more English than French, and that's the truth."

"I will take that as a compliment, Mr. Dobbins, and I am very grateful," Manella said. "Now I must go to His Lordship."

She walked out of the Kitchen and down the long corridor that led to the Study.

She knew where it was.

When she reached the hall one of the footmen went ahead of her and opened the door.

Once inside, she saw it was a very attractive room.

The pictures were all of horses, set against the soft green walls which had been one of Robert Adams' favourite colours.

The Marquis was standing in front of the fireplace which, because it was summer, was filled with flowering plants.

His eyes were on Manella as she walked towards him.

When she reached him she made a small but graceful curtsy.

"Sit down, *Mademoiselle* Chinon, which I am told is your name," he said, "and I hear too that you are French."

"I told Mr. Dobbins that my parents were French *émigrés* just before the Revolution." Manella replied. "But in fact my Father's Father was English, though his wife, my Grandmother, was French. So my Father was half-French, and I am only a quarter French."

The Marquis laughed and it broke the tension.

"But you certainly cook like a French-woman," he said, "and I enjoyed every mouthful of the five courses that were served to me."

He drew in his breath.

"Why did you not warn me what they were plotting against me?"

"I had no idea what the result of the drug would

96

be," Manella replied. "The *Comte* merely told me it would give you a *joie de vivre* and a sense of joy and delight that is often sadly missing in the English."

"What he did not say was that it would sap my will-power," the Marquis said, "and you have already told me why they wanted to do that."

"What have you . . done about the . . Priest?" Manella asked curiously.

"I told him that if he is ever seen to set foot on my land again I will have him arrested for conspiracy," the Marquis replied. " I have never seen a man run faster!"

Manella laughed.

"I have already . . heard how you have rid yourself of those . . friends."

"And that leaves you," the Marquis said, "to whom I am exceedingly grateful. Tell me, Miss Chinon, how I can thank you."

"I am actually thanking you," Manella answered, "because I was fortunate enough when I was looking for work to hear that Mrs. Wade, your Cook, had been taken ill. And I was allowed to bring with me my horse and, as you see, my dog."

Flash had been at her heels when she left the Kitchen and had come with her into the Study.

He was now lying quietly at her feet.

"If your horse is as good-looking as your dog," the Marquis said, "I shall be interested to see him."

"I love *Heron*, as I love *Flash*," Manella said, "and I was very, very thankful that we could stay here where . . no one will . . find us."

She spoke without thinking and the Marquis said quickly:

"So you are running away! I thought that might be the reason why I had the pleasure of your company!"

"Yes . . I am running . . away," Manella admitted, "but . . I do not wish to . . talk about it."

"Then we will talk about something else," the Marquis said. "Tell me what you think of my Castle."

"You must know the answer to that," Manella replied. "It is magnificent, and exactly the right background for you."

"Now you are complimenting me," the Marquis said with a twinkle in his eyes.

"How could I do anything else when you fought so gallantly under the Duke of Wellington, and have been rewarded for your services?" Manella asked.

"By becoming a Marquis?" he asked. "I think really I am more proud of being the 11th Earl."

"The next step is a Dukedom, if you want to go higher," Manella remarked.

"That is something I certainly have no wish to do," the Marquis answered. "I have had enough of fighting. I want to sleep in my own bed in my own house and ride over my own land."

"Then that is exactly what you are now able to do," Manella smiled.

There was a little pause, and she realised that the Marquis was looking at her in a way which made her feel shy.

Unexpectedly he said:

"I want to see your horse, and I feel sure he is as exceptional as his mistress and her dog. Will you ride with me tomorrow morning?"

"I would love to do that," Manella replied. "I was thinking earlier today that as you rode so early I should have to get up even earlier to exercise him so that I would not be in your way."

"You will not be that," the Marquis said, "when we ride together."

There was a little pause and they both looked at each other.

Manella had the strange feeling that they were speaking without words.

Then the Marquis said somewhat abruptly:

"I have sent grooms to tell my friends who were coming to-morrow that I unfortunately cannot be here after all to receive them."

"You did that?" Manella exclaimed. "But why?"

"Because," the Marquis said, "however careful we may be, what has happened tonight is too good a story not to be repeated over and over again by anyone who hears it."

"Yes, of course. I had not thought . . of that!" Manella murmured.

"I doubt if the French people I have just turned out will talk, but you cannot prevent servants from doing so. Any guests who come to stay tonight will bring their valets, their lady's-maids and grooms. The story will be carried back to London. That is inevitable," the Marquis said thoughtfully.

"You are very wise," Manella said. "It would certainly be a . . mistake for people to . . talk about what has . . occurred."

She thought with a little shiver that in some way even her Uncle might get to hear of it.

If he was told that the pretty Cook who had saved the Marquis's life had a horse and a dog, it would not take him long 'to put two and two together'.

She shivered again and the Marquis said:

"You are frightened! Who has frightened you and – why?"

Manella made a little gesture with her hands.

"As I have already told Your Lordship, I do not want to talk about it."

"I might be able to help you," the Marquis said. "I am usually very good at sorting out problems, and I certainly had plenty of them during the war. Why not trust me and see if I can manage to wipe away the fear in your eyes?"

She knew he was being very kind and she looked up at him gratefully before she said:

"I think . . for the moment . . I am safe . . but . . if I am not . . I will tell . . you."

"Is that a promise?" the Marquis asked.

"It is a promise!" Manella said.

She had the strange feeling that having promised him what he asked she would find it impossible not to turn to him if she was in trouble.

CHAPTER FIVE

Manella found it difficult to sleep.

It was not surprising seeing how much had happened during the evening.

She kept thinking about it, and also about the Marquis.

He had been so kind and understanding.

When she had risen to say good-night, the Marquis had said:

"What about our ride? Shall we say seven o'clock? Or is that too early for you?"

"It is not too early," Manella said, "but I ought to be preparing your breakfast."

The Marquis laughed.

"If I have to wait a few minutes after we arrive back," he said, "I will of course forgive you."

Manella walked to the door, but the Marquis got there first.

"I cannot let you go without thanking you again for saving me," he said, "from a danger I had not anticipated."

"How could you have imagined that anyone would do anything so . . wicked?" Manella enquired.

"I have always prided myself," he said, "on being a step ahead of the enemy, and using my perception. This evening I failed lamentably on both those counts, so I can only thank you once again and tell you how very, very grateful I am."

As he spoke he took her hand and lifted it to his lips.

Manella thought he would just bend over it as a Frenchman would have done.

Instead his lips actually touched her skin.

It gave her a strange feeling that ran through her like a streak of lightning.

Then because she was shy she moved away from him.

When she was outside the Study she ran towards the hall.

There was only one sleepy footman on duty, sitting in the padded chair, but he did not move when he saw her.

Manella ran up the stairs with *Flash* following her and reached her bed-room.

When she did so she felt now almost free from the terror she had felt when she was running away from her Uncle.

She walked to the window and pulled back the curtains.

The moon was shining on the lake and the stars glittered overhead.

She could not explain to herself why she suddenly felt wildly, ecstatically excited.

. . . .

Manella reached the stables at five minutes to seven.

She was really not surprised to find that the Marquis was already there.

He was choosing which horse he wanted to ride and he had already given orders for *Heron* to be saddled for her.

When, a few minutes later, they set off, going out through the back of the stables he said:

"I admire your taste in horses as much as I admire your cooking!"

"*Heron* appreciates the compliment," Manella replied, "when you have so many fine horses of your own."

"I intend to have a great many more," the Marquis said. "My last Charger in France will also be coming home to spend his years peacefully and in comfort."

Manella thought it was like him, and what she had expected, that he would love the horses which had served him.

He would make sure that they ended their days in happiness.

She knew it was something her Uncle would never think about.

The horses she had left behind at home would be sold or destroyed as soon as her Uncle could afford to replace them.

103

"You are not looking happy," the Marquis said unexpectedly. "Why?"

Manella forced herself to smile.

"I was just thinking of how many horses, after they have served their masters well, are sold to the Butcher, or just left to starve to death."

"We cannot change the world overnight," the Marquis said, "but at least we can try, each in our own small way."

It was the sort of thing, Manella thought, that he would say.

She smiled at him before he said:

"I will race you, or rather *Tempest*, which is the name of the horse I am riding, will challenge *Heron*."

They had reached some level ground. Although Manella tried in every way she could to beat him, the Marquis was half a length ahead by the time they reached the end.

"You . . won!" she managed to say breathlessly.

"And you are the best rider of any woman I have ever seen!" the Marquis answered. "Do not tell me that it is because you are French, when I know it is entirely due to your English blood!"

Manella laughed.

"That I accept, My Lord, and thank you for the compliment."

"I am merely stating a fact, " the Marquis said, "and of course I am curious to know why you are having to earn your living when you possess so fine a horse as *Heron*."

"I have already told you, it is a secret," Manella said. "I happened to arrive in the village at exactly the right moment as far as I was concerned, when your Cook had had a stroke and your Butler was frantic in case you should go hungry."

The Marquis laughed.

"I am quite certain that Dobbins thought he was dreaming when you told him you could cook."

He paused, looked at her, then said:

"And of course I am dreaming too. It is impossible that anyone could look like you, cook like you, ride like you, and yet be a human being!"

"I shall become conceited if you say such nice things to me!" Manella said, "and I know *Tempest* and *Heron* want to show you how well they can jump."

The Marquis rode ahead to where there were a number of low fences separating the fields.

Both horses sailed over them without effort and he said:

"There is a race-course on my land which I know has deteriorated, but I will certainly have it restored for use. Then we will see if *Heron* can out-jump *Tempest*, which I have a strong suspicion he will be able to do."

"It will be very exciting for him and I shall be praying hard that he succeeds." Manella said enthusiastically.

"That would be a most unfair handicap for *Tempest*," the Marquis remarked.

They laughed a great deal before they returned to the Castle.

Only as they were within sight of the stables did the Marquis say:

"It is difficult to tell you how much I have enjoyed our ride. What are you going to do for the rest of the day?"

"I have not get given it much thought," Manella replied. "Will you be alone, now that you have put off the visit of your friends?"

"I was hoping I could spend it with you," the Marquis said, "and I have a suggestion to which I hope you will agree."

Manella looked at him from under her eyelashes.

"Is that an order, or a request?"

"I always like to have things my own way," the Marquis replied.

He then told her there was a very interesting view from a special place on his estate.

It was reputed that from it one could, with the aid of a telescope or binoculars, see five Counties.

"I thought it would be amusing to take you there," he added. "We should either leave before luncheon, or else take it with us, if you would be so obliging as to get it ready."

Manella's eyes were shining at the idea.

Then she said a little hesitantly:

"You . . do not think the . . household . . will be . . shocked at you . . going driving with your . . Cook?"

"If they are, I must just put up with it," the

Marquis answered. "But I have a feeling that Dobbins and Mrs. Franklin, who was my Nanny when I was a small boy, will understand that now I have returned home I wish to share my enthusiasm for my estate with somebody – and why not you?"

"That is very plausible," Manella said teasingly, "but Your Lordship knows as well as I do that . . servants talk."

"They will talk anyway, as will the village, at my having such a pretty and clever Cook," the Marquis said, "who also has French blood in her veins!"

"That is supposedly a handicap," Manella suggested.

"As I hope to eat some more of your French dishes tonight," the Marquis said, "it is definitely, as far as I am concerned, an asset!"

When they reached the stables Manella thanked him politely and hurried back into the Castle through the Kitchen-door.

She found to her relief that Bessie and Jane had already prepared some of the dishes.

She put her riding-hat and her jacket on a chair.

Quickly she cooked the dishes and actually had three ready when Dobbins came in to say that His Lordship was in the Dining-Room.

"Ask him to start with these, Mr. Dobbins," Manella said, "and I will have the fish and the kidneys ready by the time he has finished."

Dobbins did not say anything.

She had the feeling he was thinking that his world

107

had 'turned upside down', and he would never again be surprised at anything.

Everybody had so much to say about what had happened the previous night.

They hardly seemed to notice when Manella sent a large hamper from the Kitchen to the stables.

There was another smaller one containing wine, water and coffee.

She had gone upstairs after breakfast to change from her riding-habit into one of the pretty light gowns which *Heron* had carried on his saddle.

The only difficulty was that while she had brought three gowns with her, she had not included any hats to go with them.

She was wondering what she could do when Mrs. Franklin came into the room.

"I hear His Lordship's inspecting the estate," she said, "and that you're going with him to give him his luncheon."

"That is what he has asked me to do," Manella answered.

"And quite right too!" Mrs. Franklin said to Manella's surprise. "The food they serves at the Inns round here isn't something I'd set before His Lordship! I'm certain you've arranged a good meal for him."

"I have certainly tried to do so," Manella agreed.

"Well, all I can say," Mrs. Franklin went on, "is that those who tried to trap His Lordship last night shouldn't have been allowed to sample the good food you gave them to start with! Sheer waste, that's what it was, on rats like them!"

"I agree with you," Manella said, "but remember that His Lordship enjoyed all five courses, and that is all that matters."

"You are quite right!" Mrs. Franklin said. "Anyway, if you're going now with His Lordship, you'll see some of the land that's been in the family for six generations!"

She talked possessively, and Manella understood that she and Dobbins thought of themselves as part of the family.

"I have told Bessie and Jane exactly what to do for your luncheon, Mrs. Franklin," Manella said, "and although it will be cold, I hope you will enjoy it."

"Now, don't you go worrying about us," Mrs. Franklin said. "You have a good time while you are young! Troubles come with old age – and regrets!"

She spoke wistfully.

Manella wondered if she had been unhappy with Mr. Franklin if such a person had actually existed.

She knew it was usual for Housekeepers and Cooks to be called 'Mrs.' whether they were married or not.

She made no comment, but said instead:

"Mrs. Franklin, I have no hat to wear as I rode here."

"I never thought of that," Mrs. Franklin answered. "I'm sure I could find you one later in Her late Ladyship's trunks which are all packed away upstairs in the attics. All I can suggest for the moment is that you take a sunshade."

"That is a good idea!" Manella replied. "I knew you would help me."

"I'll get the hats down just in case you want one another time," Mrs. Franklin promised, "but the sunshades are here at the end of the passage."

She went out of the room to where on the other side of the corridor were a number of doors.

Manella was already aware that it was where a great deal of the linen was kept. The sheets and pillow-cases that were used for the State Rooms were all edged with hand-made lace.

Mrs. Franklin opened a door and came back with two small sunshades.

They were just right for carrying when one was in a Phaeton.

Not too big to blow away, but large enough to keep off the sun.

Manella chose one of a pale pink with a frill round the edge.

It went very well with her gown, she thought, which was of muslin, embroidered with small field flowers.

"Of one thing I'm quite certain," Mrs. Franklin said, "you'll not see many people in this part of the world. But if you do, carry your sunshade close over your head, and it won't show that you're not wearing a hat."

"I will do that," Manella smiled, "and thank you very much."

She ran down the stairs on winged feet.

When she reached the hall she saw through the open front door that the Marquis was outside.

He was patting the horses that drew the Phaeton.

Two footmen were putting the hampers into the back of it.

The Marquis, seeing Manella approach said:

"Let me help you into the Phaeton, Miss Chinon. I hope you will not be frightened if I drive fast."

"I will try not to be, My Lord," Manella said demurely.

He helped her onto the high seat, then climbed up himself and picked up the reins.

The groom was on the single, rather precarious, seat behind them.

Then they drove off.

Manella opened her parasol and held it over her head.

"What has happened to your hat?" the Marquis enquired.

"I could not think when I was running away how *Heron* could carry it," she replied.

He drove on a little way, tooling his horses with what Manella knew was a very expert hand.

"Are you going to tell me from whom you are running away?" the Marquis asked finally, "and why?"

Manella turned to look at him.

"Please . . let me forget everything today . . and just . . enjoy myself," she begged. "I do not want to . . think about why I have come to the Castle . . or what happened . . last night. I just want to enjoy these . . fabulous horses that are pulling us . . and think of how many women would gnash their teeth if they knew I was driving alone with the Hero of Waterloo!"

The Marquis's eyes twinkled.

"Very elusive!" he said, "and clever enough to make sure that I can no longer go on fighting to win your confidence."

"Is that what you want to do?" Manella enquired.

"On the contrary," he said, "this is the sheer peace I have always wanted, driving over my own land, behind my own horses and, of course, beside the most beautiful young woman I have ever met!"

Because there was a note of sincerity in his voice, Manella blushed.

They drove for a long way, almost in silence.

Finally the Marquis brought the horses to a standstill in the centre of the wood.

To Manella's surprise she saw there was a little wooden house.

She looked at the Marquis for explanation and he said:

"This is where we had a shooting luncheon, and I think we will find it more enjoyable than sitting on the grass, or propping our backs against the trunk of a tree."

"Of course," Manella agreed, "and it is so pretty."

The Marquis told the groom to carry in the hampers and Manella unpacked them.

112

To start the meal there was some of the excellent pâté left over from last night.

After that there were wafer-thin slices of every cold meat Manella could find in the larder.

She had not forgotten to put in a most delicious French sauce, as well as a salad prepared in the French manner.

The Marquis declared it all delicious.

After that, there were several varieties of cheese including cream cheese she had made the previous day.

There were *croissants* she had cooked the night before.

They spread them with thick Jersey butter which came from one of the Marquis's farms.

The Marquis enjoyed everything, and there was champagne and a white wine to drink with the meal.

Manella then poured out the coffee.

They sat talking for a long time at an ancient oak table inside the house.

The windows were all open and the sunshine poured in.

There was only the song of the birds and the sound of small animals scuttling about outside in the undergrowth.

The groom had gone deeper into the wood where there was a pool of spring water for the horses to drink.

Manella felt as if she and the Marquis were sitting on some strange Planet in Outer Space.

The Earth, as they knew it, could not encroach on them.

There was silence for some minutes.

Then the Marquis asked:

"What are you thinking about?"

"I am thinking about you," she answered. "It is impossible to think of anything else."

"And I am just wondering how you can be so lovely and at the same time so clever. I am well aware that this picnic you have brought is very different from the picnic Mrs. Wade would have packed. Yet you talk as if you have travelled all over the world."

"Which of course I have – in my imagination, as well as through Libraries like yours," Manella replied.

"And I suppose one day some man will be lucky enough to take you to the places about which you have read, and which have become part of your dreams?"

It was really a question to which he was obviously waiting for an answer.

Manella looked away from him before she said:

"Of course . . that is what I . . hope will happen . . but so far . . I have . . not met the . . man in question."

She knew as soon as she spoke that the Marquis had tricked her into revealing if she had run away from a man.

She told herself she had been foolish not to realise that was what he was doing until it was too late.

114

She got up from the table.

"If we have much further to go to see the view you have promised me," she said, "I must pack up the luncheon."

She thought the Marquis was going to expostulate.

Instead he helped her put the dishes back into the basket and cork up what was left of the wine.

He then called to the groom to put the hampers back into the Phaeton and they set off once again.

It was doubtful if they actually saw five Counties, but the view from the top of the mound was certainly very impressive.

When they climbed down to where the horses were waiting for them Manella said:

"I thought when you were standing there you certainly were 'Monarch of All you Surveyed'! I am not surprised that you are proud of the Castle and the long history that lies behind it."

"Of course I am proud," the Marquis said. "At the same time, it has its penalties."

Manella thought he was going to tell her what those were.

Instead he seemed in a hurry to get back to the Castle.

He certainly drove very quickly.

In fact it was so quickly that it was impossible for Manella to hold up her sunshade, or even to talk.

When they arrived back the Marquis drew up his team with a flourish outside the front door.

The grooms, who were waiting for them, came hurrying to the horses' heads.

He seemed to have a lot of orders to give.

Manella therefore went into the Castle without saying anything to him.

As she went up the stairs she was thinking what an exciting day it had been.

At the same time, she was puzzled at the Marquis's behaviour on the homeward journey.

Flash had been sitting at her feet in the front of the Phaeton.

Now he was frisking about the room as if he wanted to take some exercise.

Manella put her arms round him.

"I have work to do, *Flash*," she said, "and although I would like to take you for a walk, you will have to wait until after dinner."

She found herself wondering if the Marquis would send for her as he had last night.

She wanted to talk to him; she wanted to be with him.

If he was lonely, as he would be, having put off his friends, he might find her company better than having nobody to talk to.

"He is a wonderful person," Manella murmured, "and I am so very lucky to have met him and talked to him."

Then she was frightened because she knew if she had to leave the Marquis, or he returned to London, she would miss him.

That was something she had never expected to feel.

CHAPTER SIX

Manella went slowly up the stairs to bed.

She was feeling depressed.

Since their return to the Castle the Marquis had not sent for her.

Nor had he made any suggestions about their riding tomorrow morning.

She wondered what she had done to upset him.

Or was it perhaps because he had found her boring?

In the bed-room *Flash* turned round half-a-dozen times as Setters do before he settled in his usual place by the bed.

Manella undressed, feeling somehow as if the sunshine and the moonlight were no longer with her.

She felt as if she was enveloped in a fog that she did not quite understand.

"It was so wonderful this morning," she said to herself.

She remembered how she and the Marquis had raced their horses.

Then when they had driven away from the Castle

in his Phaeton, she had thought it was the most exciting thing she had ever done.

But she now realised how attractive the *Comtesse* had been.

Perhaps the Marquis was missing her.

After the *Comtesse* he would undoubtedly find her dull and uninteresting.

The *Comtesse* had been a sophisticated and witty Frenchwoman.

Manella recalled how Dobbins had said that she had made the Marquis laugh at the things she said.

"You knows what them 'Froggies' is like," he had gone on. "I've always heard they has a double meaning to everything they says, but 'Is Lordship seemed to understand what was meant, right enough! Kept the three men in stitches, she did!"

'I suppose I should try to be like that,' Manella thought wistfully.

At the same time, whatever the Marquis had thought of the *Comtesse* in the past, he was now disillusioned.

She wondered how he could ever have been deceived by the Frenchwoman.

She had looked at the *Comte* and *Monsieur* Grave lying on the Dining-Room table.

They appeared ugly and unpleasant – especially the latter.

She could not help thinking that nobody with any sense would have trusted *Monsieur* Grave as a friend.

She had saved the Marquis, for if she had not done so, he would now be married to the *Comtesse*.

She was trying to cheer herself up on that score, but then she thought:

'Perhaps alone in his bed-room he is regretting it and is wishing he had her with him.'

She brushed her hair for some time, as her Mother had always told her to do.

Then she got into bed and blew out the candles.

In the darkness, because she felt she needed reassuring, she bent over and patted *Flash*'s head.

"You are a beautiful boy," she said. "I love you very much, and you would never disappoint me!"

She shut her eyes and started, as she always did, to say her prayers.

She was almost dropping off to sleep when she heard *Flash* give a low growl.

It was the sound he made when he sensed danger.

Manella wondered what was worrying him.

He growled again and getting to his feet walked across to the window.

"What is it, *Flash*?" Manella whispered.

She knew there was something wrong.

Although *Flash* was not barking, he was making the sound in his throat which he made when he was annoyed.

"What is the matter?" she asked.

She got out of bed and walking to where he was standing drew back the curtain.

The moonlight flooded over her in a silver stream.

Flash rose up to put his front paws on the window-ledge.

Manella looked out of the window and down to the ground.

Suddenly she was still.

Just below her she could see quite clearly there was a man.

He had started to climb up the outside of the house.

It was not a very difficult thing to do because the bricks were old and many crevices gave a foothold.

Also there were the ledges of the windows on the Ground Floor as well as the ornamentation above them.

She stared down wondering what he was doing.

It was then she saw half-hidden in the bushes on the curve of the court-yard there was a closed carriage.

Beside it, just visible in the shadows were two men.

The man was slowly climbing higher and higher.

Suddenly it dawned on Manella that he was approaching her window.

It occurred to her that he resembled *Monsieur* Grave.

With a little cry of horror she ran across the room and pulled open the door.

She ran wildly to the only person she knew who was sleeping on this floor.

The Master Suite which was occupied by the Marquis was a long way from her room.

But with *Flash* running beside her she reached it in a few seconds.

She pulled open the door and without hesitating, passed through the small hallway and opened a second door.

There was a candelabrum in the hallway so that she did not even have to search for the other door.

It led directly into the Marquis's bed-room.

Instead of being asleep the Marquis was propped up against his pillows reading a book.

As she burst into the room he looked up in astonishment.

Gasping for breath, she said:

"Th.there is a . . man . . climbing up . . outside . . my bed-room window . . it is . . *Monsieur* Grave . . I think he . . intends to . . kill me . . for what I . . did to . . them!"

The words seemed to tumble out of her mouth.

For a moment the Marquis just stared at her in sheer astonishment.

Then he put down his book and got out of bed.

"I will deal with this," he said. "Stay here and do not be frightened."

He put on a dark robe that was lying on a chair, and going to a chest-of-drawers took out a pistol.

Manella watched him wide-eyed and frightened.

She remembered now she had her Father's duelling-pistol with her, but had not thought to use it.

The Marquis walked towards the door.

"Stay here and keep *Flash* with you," he ordered.

"Please . . be careful . . he might . . hurt you," she whispered.

Even as she spoke the Marquis had gone.

She thought perhaps he had not heard her.

Because she felt weak and as if her legs would no longer carry her, she sat down on the bed.

Then she put her hands over her eyes.

As if *Flash* knew something was wrong he nuzzled against her as he did when he wanted her to pat him.

She put her arms around him.

"I am . . sure he . . wants to . . kill me, *Flash*," she said. "He and the *Comte* will . . never forgive me for . . helping the . . Marquis to escape from . . them!"

Flash seemed to understand that she was worried.

She held him close.

At the same time, she was listening.

She wondered if she would be able to hear the sound of a pistol-shot so far away.

The Marquis walked quickly down the passage towards Manella's bed-room.

He could hardly believe she was speaking the truth.

How could Grave be climbing up the outside of the house towards her room?

How was it possible that any man would dare to do such a thing when he was in the Castle?

He reached the door and found it was half-open.

His fingers tighened on the pistol.

There was no sound and he thought she must have been mistaken.

122

Perhaps she had dreamt the whole thing.

It was then he heard a movement and pushing the door open, he went in.

Manella had left the curtains drawn back.

The moonlight revealed quite clearly the open window.

A man was climbing in through the window and had one leg over the ledge.

He was moving so stealthily that the Marquis was aware he was an expert.

This was obviously not the first time he had climbed up the outside of a house to get in through a window.

The Marquis stood for a moment watching him.

Then the man slowly drew his other leg over the window-ledge.

As he did so the Marquis acted.

Raising his pistol, he shot the intruder not in the chest or the heart, which would have been easy, but deftly on the outside of his arm.

The explosion as he fired seemed to echo and re-echo round the bed-room.

At the same time the man whom the Marquis had struck gave a shrill scream and fell backwards.

Without hurrying the Marquis walked across to the window and looked down at the ground.

Below him, the man, whom he had recognised as *Monsieur* Grave had fallen 40 feet into the court-yard.

There was a flower-bed under the window and he had landed on its soft soil.

As the Marquis watched, two men appeared from the shrubbery.

Picking up the Frenchman who was now groaning with pain, they carried him to the carriage.

They were obviously afraid that they themselves might be caught.

The two horses drawing the carriage were driven away at full speed down the drive.

The Marquis watched them until they were out of sight.

Turning from the window he walked back the way he had come.

As he opened the door of his bed-room, Manella gave a cry and jumped up from the bed.

"You . . are . . safe? You are . . safe?" she asked. "They have not hurt you?"

She flung herself against him and the Marquis put his arms around her.

Just for a moment he looked down at her.

Her eyes were dark and wide with anxiety.

Her golden hair glittered in the candlelight as it fell over her shoulders and down her back.

Roughly he pulled her against him and his lips were on hers.

He kissed her as if he could not help himself, fiercely, demandingly and passionately.

To Manella, it was as if the skies had suddenly opened.

She was swept up into a Heaven she had never known existed.

As the Marquis held her closer and still closer, his lips became even more demanding.

She felt an ecstasy sweep through her that was so wonderful she knew it was love.

It was just as she had thought love would be, but far, far more marvellous.

Her whole body seemed to melt against the Marquis's so that she became a part of him.

In some way she could not understand, she was his.

He kissed her until she felt as if the room whirled about them.

She was flying in the sky and was no longer on earth.

Then the Marquis raised his head.

"What have you done to me?" he asked in a hoarse voice. "I tried to prevent this from happening, but how could I know, how could I guess, that that devil would try to intrude on you?"

"D.did you . . did you . . kill him?" Manella asked.

"No, but I wounded him," the Marquis replied, "and I promise you, he will not come back."

"I . . I thought he . . wanted to . . k.kill me." Manella murmured.

The Marquis thought, knowing Grave, he was far more likely to have wanted to kidnap her. He would prevent her from talking of what had happened.

Then he would no doubt keep her forcibly in one of the *Maisons de Plaisir* in Paris with which he was associated, and keep her drugged.

This however was not something he could say to Manella.

It was doubtful anyway if she would understand.

Even in the short time he had known her he had been aware of her innocence.

Also of her ignorance of the sophisticated world in which he had moved in Paris.

A world which he knew was also waiting for him in London.

"You are quite safe, my Darling," he said gently.

"I was . . so frightened . . for you," she murmured, "and it was . . *Flash* who . . told me that I . . was in danger."

"How can this have happened to you?" the Marquis asked.

He kissed her again until the wonder of it was almost too marvellous to bear.

She made a little incoherent sound and hid her face against his neck.

Very gently, he pulled her towards the bed.

Then he sat down and drew her close to him.

"Now listen to me, my Precious," he said. "I cannot let you run the risk of anything like this happening to you again. Although I think Grave will now return to Paris and we shall not see him again, you are too beautiful to be wandering about the world on your own."

"I do . . not want to . . wander any further," Manella said, "I . . I want to . . stay here . . with you."

The Marquis smiled.

"That is what I want too," he said, "but it is not going to be easy for me to take care of you, and therefore you have to help me."

"How . . can I . . help . . you?" Manella asked.

The Marquis drew in his breath.

"When I realised today how much I loved you," he said, "I decided I must send you away and try to forget you."

Manella gave a little cry of horror.

"But why . . why should . . you want . . to do that?"

The Marquis was silent for a moment before he said:

"Because you are so young, untouched and completely unspoilt, I thought I was doing what was best for you."

". . I do not . . understand," Manella said.

The Marquis hesitated as if he was feeling for words.

Then he said:

"I love you! I love you as I have never loved anyone before; in fact, if I tell the truth, I have never been in love before."

He saw the sudden radiance in Manella's eyes and went on quickly:

"But, my Precious, you must try to understand that I cannot ask you to marry me."

Manella was still and her eyes widened.

"I have a responsibility to my family, and my name which has been respected all down the centuries."

He saw that Manella was listening and went on:

"I must when I marry, which will not be for many, many years, marry somebody my family will accept."

Listening, Manella felt as if a cold hand had clutched at her heart and was squeezing the life-blood from it.

"What I have decided to do," the Marquis went on, "is to protect and look after you and of course, my beautiful one – to love you!"

Manella did not speak.

After a moment the Marquis said:

"I will take a small house for you in London where we can be together whenever it is possible. I have houses in other parts of the country, where no one will ask questions."

He paused before he went on:

"Now that I am home and the war is over, I shall use my Father's yacht, or else buy a new one which will carry us to enchanted lands!"

His arms drew her closer as he said:

"We will be very happy, my Darling, and I swear to you that never again will you have to work for your living. I will provide for you so that you will have plenty of money for the rest of your life."

Manella was about to speak, but it was impossible because he was kissing her.

He kissed her as if he was excited by what he was planning, and knew how happy they would be together.

He went on kissing her until it was almost impossible for her to think.

Yet she knew that she must think.

A thousand questions were trying to reach her lips, but the ecstasy the Marquis aroused in her was rising again.

All she could think of was him and the wonder of him.

His lips held her captive.

Only after a very long time did he release her and say hoarsely:

"I want to keep you with me all night telling you how much I love you. But, my Precious, I know you are tired and what has happened has been a shock. So I am going to send you back to bed!"

He kissed her forehead before he added:

"Tomorrow. Tomorrow we will talk over our plans and make them very carefully, so that no one will have the slightest idea of what is happening."

He kissed her lips.

Then resolutely, as if he ordered himself as a soldier to do his duty, he drew her across the bed-room to the little hall.

He did not open the door into the passage, but another one.

Picking up a lighted candelabrum he went ahead into a room that Manella had not seen before.

It was very large and, exquisitely furnished.

There was a huge gold carved four-poster bed that was hung with silk curtains.

"This was my Mother's room," the Marquis said softly, "and you will be safe here, my Darling, until the morning. Then I suggest you go back to your own room so that no one will know what has happened."

He did not wait for her to agree, but set the candelabrum down beside the bed.

He took her into his arms and kissed her lips not passionately but gently, as if she was infinitely precious.

"You are mine," he said softly, "and I will never lose you."

Almost before Manella could realise what was happening, he had gone from the room.

A second later she heard the door of his bed-room close.

For some minutes she could only stand staring at the closed door as if she could not believe that he had left her.

Then as she pulled back the silk cover she found that the bed was made up.

The pillow-cases were edged with lace, as were the sheets.

Knowing the excitement was all over, *Flash* settled himself down comfortably beside the bed.

Manella climbed into it, shut her eyes and tried to think of all that had happened.

The ecstasy and rapture that the Marquis had aroused in her still lingered in her breast.

At the same time, what he had just said to her was repeating itself over and over again.

It seemed to be written in letters of fire.

What he was offering her was wrong – wrong and wicked.

130

What it meant was that while she loved him with her heart and her soul, he did not really love her.

That was not the love she sought; the love which would think no sacrifice was too great.

A love a man would die for rather than lose the perfection and glory of it.

The love that was a gift from God.

As she lay in the great bed she knew what the Marquis was offering her was something cheap.

It was something her Mother would have thought of as a sin.

So would the Marquis's Mother, in whose bed she was now lying.

"I love . . him! I love . . him!" she cried in her heart.

But her mind told her that he did not love her.

She gave a sob, then the tears began to roll down her cheeks.

. . . .

It was not yet five o'clock when Manella, accompanied by *Flash*, slipped down the back stairs.

She went past the empty Kitchen to the back door and let herself out.

She had lain awake fighting with her conscience and her heart.

She felt it was as if her Mother was guiding her, and finally she knew what she must do.

"If I stay," Manella told herself, "because I love him, I shall either agree to what he suggests, or else tell him who I am."

She knew, if she did that, he would then feel obliged in honour to marry her.

But she also knew that he really had no wish to marry, as he had said, 'for many, many years'.

Just as he had no wish to be drugged and tricked into marriage by the *Comtesse*.

The candles were getting low when at last she made up her mind.

"We have to go . . away from . . here, *Flash*," she said.

Because she had spoken to him *Flash* pumped with his tail on the floor and she felt he understood.

The stables were in darkness when she reached them.

She knew that, unlike at home, there would be a groom on duty.

She opened the door nearest to *Heron*'s stall and saw by the light of the lantern hanging on the wall that most of the horses were lying down.

Heron was standing.

She put her arms round him before she looked for his saddle.

It was with his bridle suspended on the wall opposite his stall.

Deftly, because she had done it so often, she put it on his back and fastened the girths.

She tied her bundle of clothes to the back of the saddle as she had done when she left home.

As if *Heron* was pleased at the idea of going for a ride, he tossed his head and nuzzled against her.

There was still no sign of anyone.

She guessed that the place where the groom slept was at the other end of the building.

As he was doubtless young, she expected that he would sleep, as her Nanny would have said 'like a log'.

She had remembered to bring her Father's duelling-pistol with her.

She tucked it with her slippers into a pocket of the saddle.

Moving as quickly and silently as she could, she took *Heron* out into the yard.

There was a mounting-block quite near to his stall.

It took her only a second or two to settle herself onto the saddle before she picked up the reins.

With *Flash* running beside her, she went out of the stable up to the front gate which was nearest.

The first rays of the sun were just breaking in the East and the stars were beginning to fade.

As she reached the top of the drive she turned to look back at the Castle.

For one moment she asked herself why she was being so foolish as to run away when she wanted so strongly to stay.

What did it matter what she did so long as she was with the Marquis?

She only wanted to be with him, to see him and to love him with all her heart and her soul.

But she knew that what he wanted from her was not her soul.

If they were together under those terms there would always be a barrier between them.

It would eventually become unsurpassable.

It was a barrier of his making because he did not think she was good enough to be his wife.

However much she might try to deceive herself that it did not matter, she knew that sooner or later it would poison their love.

It would destroy it.

She took a last look at the Castle.

Then resolutely she rode away as quickly as she could, making for the main road.

She was running away, not only from the Marquis because of what he had suggested, but also from herself.

From a love that cried out in agony because where he was concerned she was not enough.

CHAPTER SEVEN

Manella rode down the narrow lanes which twisted and turned.

She passed through several small villages without wondering if anyone was watching her progress or not.

All she could think of was the Marquis.

She felt as if every mile that separated them was like a dagger turning in her breast.

On and on she rode.

The sun rose and it became very hot.

She thought *Heron* and *Flash* would want a drink.

It was then Manella realised that she was in a village which was much larger than those she had ridden through already.

On the far side of the village green there was a black-and-white Inn.

Outside it she saw there were several men wearing top hats.

She looked at them vaguely, then was aware they were looking at her.

She remembered, and it was like a shock, that she

was still running away from her Uncle and did not want to be seen.

She quickened *Heron*'s pace.

As soon as they were through the village and had passed the last thatched cottage she turned off the road.

There was a field sloping down to some trees at the bottom of it and she thought there would be a small stream there.

It was what she was looking for and she rode on.

She passed through a copse of silver birches until she found the stream, as she expected, just ahead of her.

She pulled *Heron* to a standstill.

As if he understood exactly why they were there, *Flash* ran into the stream, standing in it, and drinking.

Manella dismounted and tied the reins on *Heron*'s back.

"Now go and drink," she said, "You must be thirsty, and so am I, for that matter."

He went ahead of her.

Because she felt hot and tired, she took off her hat and put it down on the ground.

She had just done so when she heard the sound of a horse's hoofs.

Turning she saw a man riding through the silver birches.

For a moment he was indistinct.

Then as he came nearer she gasped.

He was wearing a black mask and as he approached

her she saw to her horror that he had a pistol in his right hand.

He rode up and pulling in his horse said in a coarse, common voice:

"Jes' wot Oi'm lookin' fer! That 'orse'll do me proud!"

Manella gave a startled cry, and moving towards *Heron* took hold of his bridle.

"You cannot take my horse," she protested.

"An' 'oo's ter stop me, Oi'd loik t'know?" the Highwayman asked.

"I will give you money," Manella said, "everything I have, but not my horse. He is mine, and I love him!"

"Oi'll luv 'im roight enough!" the Highwayman retorted. "Now, gi' me th' money, and y'can tak' this old crock in exchange."

He was looking *Heron* over as he spoke.

Then he said:

"Come on, gimme 'is reins. Oi'll change 'orses in the wood 'cross there, an' ye're lucky t'ave anyfink t'carry yer!"

"I will not let you do this!" Manella said breathlessly.

"'Ow yer goin' t'stop me?" the Highwayman asked jeeringly.

Manella knew that even if she screamed there was no one to hear her.

She wondered desperately what she could do.

The Highwayman was obviously thinking over

what she had told him because after a moment he demanded:

"Now then, gimme th' money! Moi needs be greater'n yourn."

"Unless you promise to leave me my horse, I will not give you anything!" Manella replied defiantly.

The Highwayman laughed, and it was an unpleasant sound.

"Oi needs an 'orse, an' Oi needs yer money, an' quick abaht it! Give it 'ere, or Oi'll put some lead in your dorg!"

Manella knew she was beaten.

As she gave a little murmur of horror, there was the sound of hoofs galloping towards them.

A man was coming riding through the trees.

Even before Manella could see him clearly, he must have seen the Highwayman and realised what he was doing.

He pulled a pistol from his saddle and without giving any warning shot at the Highwayman.

It would have killed him if he had not at that very moment turned round to see who was approaching.

The bullet passed over his shoulder and the Highwayman fired in return.

At the explosions of the two pistols the horses started.

The Highwayman's horse reared, almost throwing him, and so did *Heron*.

Manella was holding tightly onto his bridle.

But the Highwayman, obviously afraid of what

was happening, spurred his horse forward towards the wood.

As he rode away, Manella saw that the man who had fired at him was following him.

To her horror she saw it was her Uncle.

He was swaying in a strange way in the saddle as he disappeared amongst the trees.

Too frightened to know what to do, or even for the moment to move, she could only stare at the point where the two horses had disappeared.

Then there came another shot that seemed to reverberate through the air.

As Manella held tightly onto *Heron* as if for protection, yet another horse appeared, this time from the direction that she had come.

With a leap of her heart she saw it was the Marquis.

He rode up to her at a gallop.

He flung himself from his horse and put his arms round her.

"Are you all right?" he asked. "You have not been hurt?"

For a moment, it was impossible for Manella to speak.

She could only cling to the Marquis knowing that because he was there *Heron* was saved.

She knew too that she wanted the Marquis more than she had ever wanted anything in the whole of her life.

"My Darling, my sweet!" the Marquis was saying.

"How could you leave me? How could you go away like that?"

He pulled her closer before he went on:

"Forgive me, you have to forgive me, for being a pompous prig. I know now that I cannot live without you, and I want to marry you immediately."

She looked up at him in amazement, finding it hard to believe that he was saying the words she so much wanted to hear.

She was not quite certain she was not imagining it.

Her eyes were full of tears and her lips were trembling.

The Marquis looked down at her, thinking no woman could look more lovely.

Then he said softly:

"I will ask you properly, hoping that you will forgive me. Will you, my lovely, precious, perfect little Angel, do me the great honour of becoming my wife?"

He spoke solemnly, but he did not wait for an answer.

His lips were on hers, and he kissed her wildly, passionately, demandingly.

Manella felt this must be a dream and could not really be happening.

How was it true?

After her running away and being so frightened by the Highwayman, was the Marquis really there and asking her to be his wife?

It was so wonderful and at the same time extraordinary!

She felt herself trembling against him and had the strange feeling he was trembling too.

He raised his head and said in a hoarse voice:

"I thought I had lost you! I saw you going down the drive as the dawn broke and could not believe that you were really leaving me. I had thought conceitedly that you loved me."

"I . . I do . . love you," Manella said in a whisper, "but I . . knew it was . . wrong to do . . what you wanted."

"Completely and absolutely wrong!" the Marquis said positively. "And I realised as I watched you go that I had destroyed my only real hope of happiness."

He kissed her again as if it was easier to tell her what she meant to him without words.

They clung together.

Then Manella saw a horse coming out of the wood.

As it drew nearer she gave an exclamation.

"It is *Magpie*!"

The Marquis, who had his back to the approaching horse, turned his head.

"How do you know?" he asked. "Surely that is not the horse the Highwayman was riding?"

Even as he spoke, *Magpie* reached them and *Heron* whinnied as if greeting him.

It was then the Marquis realised that the two horses looked very much alike.

The new horse was as well bred as *Heron*.

Manella went to *Magpie* and patted him on the neck.

She saw that the reins hung loose and she knotted them at his neck.

The Marquis watched her for a moment.

Then he asked:

"As you seem to know that horse, perhaps you would tell me to whom it belongs?"

Manella drew in a deep breath.

"I.It belongs to my Uncle," she said. "It is he from whom I am . . running . . away . . and if . . *Magpie* has unseated him . . I must . . get away . . at once."

As she spoke, her voice trembling, she looked in the direction from which *Magpie* had come.

There was no sign of her Uncle.

Then as if she suddenly realised she need no longer be afraid, she moved closer to the Marquis.

"Will you . . tell him that . . I am . . staying with you . . and that . . we are . . going to . . be m.married?"

She spoke the words slowly and tentatively as if she was half-afraid they might not be true.

"I will tell him you belong to me," the Marquis answered, "and I cannot imagine he will object to our marriage."

It flashed through Manella's mind that if she married the Marquis, her Uncle would not find it at all easy to blackmail him into paying his debts.

There was however no point in saying so.

She could only pray that somehow the Marquis would prevent her Uncle from bullying her.

And most of all, from having to marry the old Duke of Dunster.

It all seemed confused and unreal in her mind after the shock of what had just occurred.

But there was also the wonder and ecstasy of knowing that the Marquis really loved her.

He had asked her to marry him without knowing who she was.

As if he understood what she was thinking, the Marquis said gently:

"Leave everything to me. I will go and see what has happened to your Uncle, while you take charge of the horses."

He kissed her first as if he could not help himself.

Mounting his horse, he rode towards the wood.

Manella watched him go.

Then she was saying a prayer of gratitude because he loved her.

At the same time, it was a cry for help in case her Uncle should be unpleasant.

Worst of all, his behaviour might be so repulsive that the Marquis would regret having asked her to be his wife.

"Help . . me . . God . . help me . . Mama!" she begged. "The Marquis has . . found me and he really . . loves me! Please . . oh . . please . . do not let . . anything . . spoil it . . now!"

The two horses were cropping the grass.

Flash was again standing in the stream as if he still wanted to cool himself.

Manella moved instinctively a little way towards the wood into which the Marquis had vanished.

She was still praying.

She was so afraid that at any moment he might appear with her Uncle and that he was determined to make trouble.

After what seemed to her a very long time, she saw the Marquis returning.

He was alone!

As he came through the trees she could not look at his face, afraid of what she would see there.

She just stood waiting.

He reached her, dismounted and put his arms around her.

He held her close, but he did not kiss her.

After a moment Manella asked in a voice he could hardly hear:

"W.What . . has h.happened?"

"I am afraid, my darling," the Marquis replied, "that your Uncle is dead!"

"D.Dead?" Manella could hardly repeat the word.

"The Highwayman had shot him through the heart," the Marquis explained, "and there was another wound on his shoulder where he must have hit him the first time he fired."

Manella shut her eyes and hid her face against his shoulder.

"There is nothing we can do for him now," the Marquis said quietly, "and because I do not want

144

you to be upset, I think it would be best if we went straight to the Chief Constable, who was a friend of my Father's, and tell him exactly what has occurred."

"Y.you do not . . want to move . . Uncle Herbert's body?" Manella asked.

"No," the Marquis said firmly. "I do not want you to be upset by seeing him and, as I have already told you, there is nothing we can do. The bullet passed through his heart. He would have died instantly."

He did not wait for Manella to reply, but lifted her onto *Heron*'s back.

Then he untied the reins she had knotted on *Magpie*'s neck.

Leading him, he mounted *Tempest* and started to ride back through the trees towards the village.

Flash followed.

Manella thought it was significant that for the first time since she had run away there was no need for her to hurry.

She looked at the Marquis and he smiled at her.

"I love and adore you!" he said softly, "and when we get back to the Castle, I will be able to tell you how much."

She smiled back at him.

As they rode on she thought that the sun had never been more golden.

With the Marquis beside her, it was as if they were riding to Paradise.

As they approached the village there seemed to

be no one about except for some children playing happily on the green.

To her surprise, the Marquis stopped.

"I want to thank you," he said to them, "for being so clever as to tell me where this lady had gone, and that there was a Highwayman hiding among the trees. Go now and buy yourselves all the sweets you want, and here is the money to pay for them."

He took a purse from his pocket and gave each of the smaller children a half-sovereign piece.

To the older ones he gave a guinea.

They stared down at the money in their hands as if mesmerised, and far too excited to thank him.

They rode on and Manella said in a small voice:

"If they . . had not told you . . where . . I was . . the Highwayman . . would have . . taken *Heron* . . from me."

"Your Uncle might have prevented it," the Marquis said, "but I cannot understand why, when he had his pistol in his hand, he did not at least disable the Highwayman."

"Papa always said that Uncle Herbert was not a good shot!" Manella replied. "It annoyed him that his brother preferred London to the country."

"I do not think I have ever seen your Uncle before," the Marquis remarked.

He was thinking as he spoke that he looked an unpleasant individual.

He could well understand why Manella had been so frightened of him.

They rode on in silence for a while until the Marquis said:

"The Chief Constable lives only about a mile from here, so we will call on him on our way to the Castle. You must tell me, my precious one, what is your Uncle's name and, if, as I suspect, you are not Miss Chinon, what is yours."

Manella gave a little laugh.

"It seems . . strange . . but very . . wonderful . . that you really want to . . marry me . . not knowing who I am."

"I knew as I saw you going down the drive at dawn this morning that if you were the Devil's daughter, I would still want to make you my wife!" the Marquis replied.

Manella drew in her breath.

"If you only . . knew how . . much I have . . longed to hear you say . . that!"

"Now tell me who you are," the Marquis ordered, "and what is the name of your Uncle."

"He . . was the 7th . . Earl of Avondale," Manella whispered. "He was . . Papa's brother . . and inherited the title because . . I was the only child."

Manella hesitated before continuing:

"I was running away from him because, being in debt, he was trying to force me to marry a rich old man, the Duke of Dunster."

The Marquis stared at her in sheer astonishment.

"But – I knew your Father when I was a boy!" he exclaimed. "My Father was very fond of him. Why did you not tell me?"

Manella turned away from him and did not reply.

"I know the answer," the Marquis said. "Because you were hiding you called yourself by a French name."

"I.it was my . . Grandmother's name," Manella explained.

"And when I offered you my protection," the Marquis said slowly, as if he was working it out, "you thought I did not really love you."

Again there was nothing Manella could say.

The Marquis drew his horse a little nearer to hers.

"It was incredibly stupid of me," he said, "not to know that any woman as perfect as you must have come from a family the equal of my own."

He paused before he added:

"I can only say that I am utterly ashamed of myself for my lack of perception in not realising how unique and wonderful you are, and for thinking even for a moment that I could be happy without you as my wife."

The way he spoke was very moving and Manella said:

"Please . . do not let . . us talk . . about it any . . more. I love you . . and now that you . . love me I am so happy that I . . feel I want to . . fly like a bird."

There was a note of rapture in her voice and she added:

"I want . . to forget . . everything that has . . frightened me."

"I will make sure of that!" the Marquis promised.

Because of the way he was looking at her, Manella felt her heart turn over in her breast.

. . . .

Later that night, Manella lay once again in the big gold-canopied bed that had always been occupied by the Marchionesses of Buckingdon.

She was waiting for her husband to come through the communicating door.

It was difficult to believe that she really was married.

The Marquis had arranged everything.

He had seen the Chief Constable who had told him not to worry.

He would send his men to find the Earl's body and have it taken to the Church at Avondale to await burial.

It was as they were riding back that the Marquis said:

"You know, my Precious, that the only sensible thing for us to do is be married immediately; in fact this very evening."

Manella looked at him in astonishment and he explained:

"Your Uncle, appalling though I realise he was, had become on your Father's death the Head of the Family. All your relations must be notified in case they wish to attend the Funeral."

He paused for a moment as if he was thinking it out, before he went on:

"That means we cannot be together in the same house without a chaperon. It will be expected that

149

many months of mourning must pass before I can make you my bride."

"I . . I do not . . want to . . leave you," Manella said softly.

"It is something I will never allow you to do," the Marquis answered, "and as my Chapel is private and the Vicar of the Parish is my Chaplain, I can marry without the necessity of a Special Licence."

Manella was aware that this applied to a number of Chapels.

The one in Mayfair was notorious for the number of marriages which took place there.

As they rode side by side the Marquis put out his hand.

"Will you marry me at once, my Darling?" he asked. "Otherwise we may have to wait a long time before we can go on our honeymoon. Not that it would matter where we were, so long as we could be together."

Manella felt his fingers press hers, and she said:

"I would be happy with you on . . top of the . . Himalayas, or at the bottom of the . . sea."

The Marquis laughed.

"I cannot promise you a journey to the bottom of the sea, but I will certainly take you to India, as well as to a great number of other places where I will tell you of my love."

He paused and added softly:

"We will be certain we have been there before in another life."

"That . . is what . . I believe too," Manella said,

"but I never . . imagined I would . . find somebody
. . who . . thought the way . . I do."

"We think the same, our love is the same, and we
are one and the same!" the Marquis declared.

As the Castle came in sight Manella said:

"I suppose you realise that I have very few clothes
with me, and I am afraid you will find me not at all
smart. I . . shall compare very . . unfavourably with
the . . elegant ladies . . who have . . amused you in
. . Paris and . . London."

"Whatever you wear you look beautiful, and I will
see nothing but your eyes and your lips," the Marquis replied. "However I am already planning to
send Watson to London tomorrow to tell all the top
Dressmakers to bring us their prettiest gowns for
you to choose from."

"Will . . they really . . agree to come?" Manella
asked.

"I will be very surprised if they do not jump at the
chance," the Marquis said, his eyes twinkling.

"Of course! I had forgotten how . . important you
are!" Manella exclaimed.

The Marquis thought it was something no other
woman would have forgotten and he understood
what Manella meant.

She loved him simply as a man, and that was how
he had always wanted to be loved.

And he loved her because he had never met
anyone like her.

She was pure, unspoilt and, in every way he could
think of, completely perfect.

When they arrived back at the Castle, he took her up to his Mother's bed-room.

"This is yours," he said, "and, my Precious, no Countess has ever been as beautiful as the first Marchioness will be."

"As long as . . you think I am . . beautiful," Manella said, "nothing . . else matters."

He kissed her tenderly, then left her.

The Housekeeper was wildly excited by the information that they were to be married and produced all sorts of things to make Manella feel like a bride.

The Marquis's Chaplain arrived at half-past-six.

By that time, Manella was dressed in her own white muslin gown.

But she wore a magnificent Brussels lace veil, and a large tiara of diamonds.

She was told it had been worn by the last six Countesses.

Her bouquet was of orchids and lilies which came from the greenhouse.

When the Marquis brought her to the Chapel, she saw that it was decorated with the same flowers.

The only witnesses were Mrs. Franklin and Dobbins and, of course, *Flash*.

It was obvious the two servants both felt very honoured to be allowed to take part in the proceedings.

After the marriage had taken place, during which Manella felt that the angels were singing, they went up to her *Boudoir*.

It was a lovely room she had not seen before.

There were three long windows to illuminate the

many treasures which successive Châtelaines of the Castle had accumulated.

It was decorated with the same flowers that were in her bouquet and her bed-room.

She thought that the Gardeners must have emptied the Conservatory and the greenhouses.

They toasted themselves in champagne during a light dinner.

Manella guessed it had been made with the greatest difficulty, but with a loving endeavour, by Bessie and Jane, and doubtless all the rest of the household.

It was not a French meal, but very palatable.

She knew however that both she and the Marquis would feel that anything at this moment would taste like the ambrosia of the gods.

When the meal was over the Marquis drew her into the bed-room.

Manella had removed her veil and tiara before dinner.

Now the Marquis removed the pins from her hair so that it fell over her shoulders.

He pulled her into his arms and kissed her.

She felt a wild excitement sweep through her.

He undid the buttons of her gown without releasing her lips.

Then he raised his head and said, with a voice that was very deep:

"Get into bed, my wonderful wife."

A little later he came into the room and sitting down on the side of the bed he looked down at her.

153

"Are you real?" he asked.

"That is .. what I was .. about to ask you," Manella answered. "I am .. so afraid that this is a .. dream and I will .. wake up to find I am still .. running away from .. Uncle Herbert .. because of his determination to make me .. marry the .. Duke!"

"Instead you are married to me!" the Marquis said. "And just as I know I am the first man ever to have kissed you, my Precious, I know there will never be any other man in your life."

He got into the bed beside her as he spoke and took her into his arms.

"I love you so desperately," he said, "and so overwhelmingly, that I am afraid of frightening you, or hurting you."

Manella was quivering because his hands were touching her.

Then as he kissed her eyes, her cheeks, her mouth, her neck and the softness of her breasts she knew that she was in Heaven.

She felt the warmth of the sun and the shining of the stars in her breast.

The moonlight too was moving through her body and she was no longer human.

Then as the Marquis made her his very gently and lovingly, together they touched the peaks of ecstasy.

Other books by Barbara Cartland

Romantic Novels, over 500, the most recently published being:

The Angel and the Rake
The Queen of Hearts
The Wicked Widow
To Scotland and Love
Love and War
Love at the Ritz
The Dangerous Marriage
Good, Or Bad?
This is Love!
Seek the Stars
The Dream and the Glory
(In aid of the St. John Ambulance Brigade)

Running Away to Love
Look with the Heart
Safe in Paradise
Love in the Ruins
A Coronation of Love
A Duel of Jewels
The Duke is Trapped
The Wonderful Dream
Love and a Cheetah
Drena and the Duke

Autobiographical and Biographical:

The Isthmus Years 1919–1939
The Years of Opportunity 1939–1945
I Search for Rainbows 1945–1976
We Danced All Night 1919–1929
Ronald Cartland (With a foreword by Sir Winston Churchill)
Polly – My Wonderful Mother
I Seek the Miraculous

Historical:

Bewitching Women
The Outrageous Queen (The Story of Queen Christina of Sweden)
The Scandalous Life of King Carol
The Private Life of Charles II
The Private Life of Elizabeth, Empress of Austria
Josephine, Empress of France
Diane de Poitiers
Metternich – The Passionate Diplomat
A Year of Royal Days
Royal Jewels
Royal Eccentrics
Royal Lovers

Sociology:

You in the Home	Etiquette
The Fascinating Forties	The Many Facets of Love
Marriage for Moderns	Sex and the Teenager
Be Vivid, Be Vital	The Book of Charm
Love, Life and Sex	Living Together
Vitamins for Vitality	The Youth Secret
Husbands and Wives	The Magic of Honey
Men are Wonderful	The Book of Beauty and Health

Keep Young and Beautiful by Barbara Cartland and Elinor Glyn
Etiquette for Love and Romance
Barbara Cartland's Book of Health

General:

Barbara Cartland's Book of Useless Information with a
   Foreword by the Earl Mountbatten of Burma.
   (In aid of the United World Colleges)
Love and Lovers (Picture Book)
The Light of Love (Prayer Book)
Barbara Cartland's Scrapbook
   (In aid of the Royal Photographic Museum)
Romantic Royal Marriages
Barbara Cartland's Book of Celebrities
Getting Older, Growing Younger

Verse:

Lines on Life and Love

Music:

An Album of Love Songs
sung with the Royal Philharmonic Orchestra.

Films:

A Hazard of Hearts
The Lady and the Highwayman
A Ghost in Monte Carlo
A Duel of Hearts

Cartoons:

Barbara Cartland Romances (Book of Cartoons)
has recently been published in the U.S.A., Great Britain,
and other parts of the world.

Children:

A Children's Pop-Up Book: "Princess to the Rescue"

Cookery:

Barbara Cartland's Health Food Cookery Book
Food for Love
Magic of Honey Cookbook
Recipes for Lovers
The Romance of Food

Editor of:

"The Common Problem" by Ronald Cartland (with a preface by
the Rt. Hon. the Earl of Selborne, P.C.)
Barbara Cartland's Library of Love
Library of Ancient Wisdom
"Written with Love" Passionate love letters selected by Barbara
Cartland

Drama:

Blood Money
French Dressing

Philosophy:

Touch the Stars

Radio Operetta:

The Rose and the Violet
(Music by Mark Lubbock) Performed in 1942.

Radio Plays:

The Caged Bird: An episode in the life of Elizabeth Empress of
Austria. Performed in 1957.

A List of Barbara Cartland Titles Available from Mandarin

While every effort is made to keep prices low, it is sometimes necessary to increase prices at short notice. Mandarin Paperbacks reserves the right to show new retail prices on covers which may differ from those previously advertised in the text or elsewhere.

The prices shown below were correct at the time of going to press.

☐	7493 1249 1	**Born of Love**	£3.50
☐	7493 0814 1	**A Dynasty of Love**	£2.99
☐	7493 0810 9	**The Earl Rings a Belle**	£2.99
☐	7493 1243 2	**Hidden by Love**	£2.99
☐	7493 0798 6	**Hiding**	£2.99
☐	7493 0800 1	**Just Fate**	£2.99
☐	7493 1240 8	**A Kiss in Rome**	£2.99
☐	7493 1284 X	**Look with the Heart**	£3.50
☐	7493 1285 8	**Love in the Ruins**	£3.50
☐	7493 0803 6	**Love Lifts the Curse**	£2.99
☐	7493 0813 3	**Love Strikes Satan**	£2.99
☐	7493 1241 6	**Loved for Himself**	£2.99
☐	7493 0745 5	**Magic from the Heart**	£2.99
☐	7493 1242 4	**No Disguise for Love**	£2.99
☐	7493 0805 2	**The Queen saves a King**	£2.99
☐	7493 0802 8	**A Tangled Web**	£2.99
☐	7493 0744 7	**A Theatre of Love**	£2.99
☐	7493 1248 3	**This is Love**	£3.50
☐	7493 0743 9	**Too Precious to Lose**	£2.99
☐	7493 0746 3	**Two Hearts from Hungary**	£2.99
☐	7493 0815 X	**Warned by a Ghost**	£2.99
☐	7493 0799 4	**The Windmill of Love**	£2.99

All these books are available at your bookshop or newsagent, or can be ordered direct from the address below. Just tick the titles you want and fill in the form below.

Cash Sales Department, PO Box 5, Rushden, Northants NN10 6YX.
Fax: 0933 410321 : Phone 0933 410511.

Please send cheque, payable to 'Reed Book Services Ltd.', or postal order for purchase price quoted and allow the following for postage and packing:

£1.00 for the first book, 50p for the second; **FREE POSTAGE AND PACKING FOR THREE BOOKS OR MORE PER ORDER.**

NAME (Block letters) ....

ADDRESS ....

....

☐ I enclose my remittance for ....

☐ I wish to pay by Access/Visa Card Number

Expiry Date

Signature ....

Please quote our reference: MAND